KT-424-446

Alan Gibbons

Alan Gibbons is a full time writer and a visiting speaker and lecturer at schools, colleges and literary events nationwide, including the major Book Festivals. He lives in Liverpool with his wife and four children.

Alan Gibbons has twice been shortlisted for the Carnegie Medal, with *The Edge* and *Shadow of the Minotaur*, which also won the Blue Peter Book Award in the 'Book I Couldn't Put Down' category.

WS 2245954 5

CR
F
GIB

Blood Pressure

ALAN GIBBONS

A Dolphin
Paperback

First published in Great Britain in 2005
as a Dolphin paperback
by Orion Children's Books
a division of the Orion Publishing Group Ltd
Orion House
5 Upper St Martin's Lane
London WC2H 9EA

Copyright © Alan Gibbons 2005

The moral right of Alan Gibbons to be identified as the
author of this work has been asserted.

All rights reserved. No part of this publication may be
reproduced, stored in a retrieval system, or transmitted,
in any form or by any means, electronic, mechanical,
photocopying, recording or otherwise, without the prior
permission of Orion Children's Books.

A catalogue record for this book is
available from the British Library

Typeset at The Spartan Press Ltd,
Lymington, Hants

Printed in Great Britain by
Clays Ltd, St Ives plc

ISBN 1 84255 199 X

www.orionbooks.co.uk

To Bob and Brenda Swindells

PART ONE
Blood Pressure

One

There was pressure above his eyes. Half in, half out of sleep, he let out a low groan.

'Aidan.'

It was Mum's voice he heard, distant, as if eddying through metres of dark water, getting lost in gluey currents. He was unable to rise towards it, however. The dream held him fast in its grasp. That dream, the one that never went away. There, beyond the black fathoms of sleep, he was a small boy again, caught in a downpour, running along the slick, grey pavement. Mum grabbed for his hand but he wriggled free. She was calling him back, her voice echoing through the roar of the rain. He wasn't paying any attention. He wanted to see Dad. He loved his dad. He loved the way he came in and threw him high in the air before catching him again. Dad was in that house.

They'd spotted him from the street corner.

'Aidan, are you OK?'

Mum's voice quivered a moment, opening a window in the gloom, then swam away from him. Aidan was that little boy again. He ran indoors. The house creaked around him, seeming to sag under the weight of the heaving wind. His heart was pattering with unease at the strange surroundings, but he ran on. He was aware of Mum following. At the end of the hallway the door stood open, a slash of darkness beyond. What was Dad doing there? Then there was another voice, an angry voice. Somebody was in there with Dad. Warring voices boomed off the walls. Was this man trying to hurt his Daddy? A sliver of ice gouged his insides.

Stop it. Don't hurt him!

'Aidan!'

He turned towards Mum's voice but the dream was thick around him like fog, drawing him back to a time when she was younger. Then she stopped, that younger self, seeing something. The boy glimpsed her expression, wide eyes, mouth twisted in horror. The face he knew so well seemed to fade leaving nothing but fear. The way her hands flew to that pale, dissolving face made him scream. Then he had the impression of something roaring, spitting fire. The explosion seemed to suck the air out of the room. After that something loomed in the rolling smoke, a white figure crucified on a cross of flame. A scream of agony flew past the terrified boy, then there was a heavy thud as something fell to the floor.

'Aidan, wake up!'

Mum was shaking him.

'Wha . . . ?'

The shaking went on.

'You're having a nightmare.'

Mum had one hand on his sleeve, the other on the steering wheel. He knuckled his eyes, then realising it made him look like a little kid, he sat up. It was a nightmare all right, the one he'd been having on and off for longer than he dared remember. There had been times, when he was younger, that he'd hardly dared close his eyes in case that white figure came lurching out of the shadows, the cry of anguish exploding past him into the

4

darkness. Aidan had told Mum about it once or twice but that was years ago. It seemed to upset her so he didn't mention it any more. Mum flashed a look his way then turned her eyes back to the motorway.

'Aidan, you're staring at me.'

'Oh sorry.'

It was all to do with the nightmare. He still half expected to see the wide eyes, the shocked look, but that was the mother in his dream. At last he was back. It was Wednesday. It was July. It was wet. A fragment of forgotten dream ached behind his eyes, then it began to evaporate. Nothing remained except its bleak after-taste.

'Where are we?' Aidan asked.

They were cresting a rise. Below there was lush countryside. Aidan had dropped off somewhere around Birmingham. This wasn't Birmingham. Mist curtained the trees. Ahead, thousands of tiny lights winked in the gloom of early evening. A city was beckoning. The only sound was the rumble of the car's engine and the beat of the windscreen wipers.

'We're on the Thelwall Viaduct,' Mum said, indicating the huge concrete structure, grey pillars stained by the downpour.

'Not far now.'

Not far. Not far from Liverpool. Now fully awake, the nightmare's barbs loosening from the flesh of his mind, Aidan had the strangest feeling something was waiting there for him. Some instinct he didn't understand alerted him to the gravitational force of events far in the past. Maybe there had always been clues, things unsaid as much as things said, spaces in his life that he couldn't quite explain.

Sometimes you know, just know, your life has changed. The second hand of the clock seems to shudder as if splicing together two kinds of time. There is the zone in which you live. Within it everything seems normal. Then there is another place, out there in the shadows. That's what was happening to Aidan that rain-drenched night in the north west of England: he was coming out of the known. Even as they drove, the landscape of his life was being re-made.

It was just the two of them in the car: Mum silent now at the wheel, Aidan still a little drowsy in the passenger seat next to her. Radio 2 was on low, Mum's choice not Aidan's. By the time they left the gridlock of the M6 and joined the M62, weaving through the tangle of road works, Aidan felt he'd crossed a kind of Rubicon and yes, he did know enough Roman history to understand what that meant. The fabric of things had changed and changed utterly. After all, he had an appointment with a dead man.

He looked up at the inky storm clouds. He felt exhausted despite his sleep. The dream, that vapour of fantasy, memory and obsession, had all but faded but its power still lingered, fingers of unease jabbing through his brain. His temple throbbed.

It was pressure.

Blood pressure.

'Mum,' he said, 'I'm sorry about earlier.'

'Forget it,' she said.

'No, I am. I know you've got a lot on your mind.'

What she had on her mind was Granddad. They'd just got the news. His illness had taken a turn for the worse. So what had Aidan done when Mum said they had to go up to Liverpool for a few days? He'd only thrown a wobbler.

'But I had plans!' he'd complained.

He had plans, all right, and they all concerned himself. School was out and he'd been looking forward to the long summer nights hanging out with his friends.

'I was thoughtless.'

It was a good word. Admitting to thoughtlessness was usually enough to neutralise his parents' anger. What you might call a pre-emptive strike. Mum checked her mirrors and pulled into the middle lane to overtake a lorry.

'Aidan, you're fifteen. You're supposed to be thoughtless. It goes with the territory.'

He'd hoped she was going to say no, he wasn't thoughtless at all, but maybe that was expecting too much. Instead, she whittled him down to size with her amateur psychology. Sure, like you remember what it's like to be fifteen! Mum was always coming out with things like that, her being a teacher. Like she said, goes with the territory.

'I just wish there was a different way, Aidan, but there isn't.'

'You could have left me home,' he interrupted. 'I'm nearly sixteen, for goodness' sake.'

Mum answered in a flash.

'You're fifteen and a quarter and no way am I going to leave you in the house on your own.'

Maybe she decided that she'd spoken more sharply than she intended because she immediately added:

'Look, I know how much you were looking forward to your holidays.'

Oh no you don't, Aidan thought. You haven't seen Emily Gardner.

'But your Gran and Granddad need me. This week of all weeks your father has to be in Singapore.'

Singapore. Business. Aidan imagined his dad on the plane, tapping away at the laptop, playing with sales figures, projections, orders.

'What with Pat living over in the States,' Mum went on, 'it's down to me to be here for them.'

Pat was Mum's older sister, Aidan's aunt. She lived in

North Carolina, married to a doctor, a big cheese in something-paedics.

'Mum and Dad are going through a bad time, Aidan. Right now, we're all they've got. You understand that, don't you?'

'Of course I do.'

Aidan wasn't sure he sounded convincing. He still couldn't believe all his plans for the summer were wrecked. Emily had the best legs in the whole year and she'd agreed to go out with him. Now anybody could step in. There were more than enough predators in Year Ten to keep him on his toes. But Dad was away on business in the Far East and Aunty Pat was in the States and he, as Mum had so precisely reminded him, was fifteen and a quarter so he had to accompany her to Liverpool. It stunk being a teenager. Three more years and he'd be at uni and free. He slumped back in his seat and watched the suburbs of the city stutter by.

He noticed kids in silver Puffa jackets, hoodies, baseball caps, sheltering in the doorways of boarded-up and shuttered shops. A yellow police van with CCTV slowly cruised past them then accelerated away to hoots and whistles. Aidan watched the lash of the rain, the bleary glare of headlights. Liverpool.

As they turned the corner into Elmwood Street where his grandparents lived he wasn't thinking about Granddad's illness at all. He was mourning his lost summer and Emily's legs. He saw the glow of the streetlamps, heard the slapping wiper blades and felt the foreignness of the place. Then he froze. He had glimpsed a girl in a doorway. He only saw her for a moment but he was left with an impression: full, red lips; a wisp of black hair; and brown eyes that met his gaze in a way that was bold, almost confrontational. The moment Mum stopped the car he got out

8

and looked back up the street, at the doorway, the dripping darkness. He saw a few blurry forms in the rain but the girl had gone. He knew right away he had to meet her again.

Two

Every story, so they say, has a beginning, a middle and an end. Only you don't always start at the beginning, and things have a habit of carrying on way past the end. You think you know where the story starts, but you don't. There can be a back story, the stuff that was hanging about before the beginning. Baggage. When Aidan woke up next morning in crisp white sheets, with the sun on his face, he was living for the moment. He had no idea what had come before, or what was lying in wait for him just around the corner. He didn't know his family had any baggage.

The air was warming up, turning humid and sticky. He glanced at his watch. Ten o'clock. Mum had let him lie in, which was a novelty in itself. For a good Catholic girl, she had a strong Protestant work ethic. He swung his feet out of bed and sat up. That's when he remembered. The previous evening. Gran had been on form, killing the fatted calf. Should she warm some pea and ham soup? No. Did he want a sandwich then? No. Did he want a slice of her chocolate cake? No. But he'd always liked her chocolate cake. Yes Gran, when he was five! Then it was: did he have a girlfriend? Yes, he did. Was he still doing well at school? Yes, he was. Why did she have to witter on?

Then he saw Granddad and he knew why. His eyes were bloodshot and the whites were yellowish. They were swimming from lack of sleep. Gran had good reason to fuss. It took her mind off his illness. The moment she stopped, she would fall apart. Aidan knew that, he felt the hurt, it was a living thing that filled the room, but he couldn't find anything to say. He couldn't make a connection. He just felt so cold towards them, blaming them for his lost summer. And he hated himself for it. So he cut and run. He shot them a curt *going to bed*, then retreated upstairs. Mum wasn't going to be impressed. Best behaviour, that's what she'd asked for, a bit of effort. So what did he do? He'd had the dutiful grandson routine all prepared and, when it came to it, he just couldn't deliver. He'd messed up.

Sitting on the bed the morning after, enjoying the breeze on his skin, he thought through a plan of sorts. He was going to shower, dress and slip out of the house, hopefully unnoticed. He had a street map of Liverpool. He might as well make the best of his northern exile. After all, some people had this down as a cool place to be. Aidan couldn't see it but he wasn't going to find out stewing in the house. Ten minutes later he was heading for the front door. Gran saw him.

'Don't you want any breakfast?' she asked.

Aidan shook his head and opened the door.

'Not yet,' he grunted and closed it behind him.

What he really meant was: not here. Not in the death house. He'd spotted a supermarket on the dual carriageway. They were bound to have a café. He'd eat there. It meant paying for it himself, but so what? He was making a point. He didn't want to be there, in that house. He didn't want to talk about his girlfriend and whether she was 'nice'. He didn't want to talk about school. He didn't want to talk about illness and death. He was fifteen. He should be out having fun.

Death was for later.

Much later.

Once he was on the street he started breathing more easily. He wouldn't have to face Mum for a few hours. He wouldn't have to put up with old people furniture and old people talk. He could be himself, even if it meant being on his own. He looked around for the girl from the night before. She wasn't there. Then he remembered what Mum had told him. The Liverpool schools broke up a week later than his did. She'd be in class. He was disappointed, but at least he had the streets to himself. He sucked in a lungful of air. There was a taste of petrol fumes but, hey, this wasn't half bad. OK, so he wasn't with his friends but he could do as he liked. He didn't have anybody breathing down his neck.

He was free.

The supermarket café was nearly empty too, which was a plus. It also did breakfasts until half past eleven, which was even better. He ordered the works and found a table in the corner, out of the sun. He munched egg-drenched toast and watched the other diners. An old woman in Hush Puppies was slowly sipping a mug of tea and staring straight ahead. At the far end of the café there were four men in their twenties. They were wearing shorts and tee-shirts, all grimed with muck. There were copies of the *Sun* and the *Star* on the table, lobotomy comics. They must be building workers or some such, Aidan guessed. Two young mums made up the numbers. They were busy scooping their toddlers out of metal shopping trolleys and into red and yellow plastic high chairs. Clearing the tables was a girl in a blue apron, green tee-shirt and blue and green baseball cap. She had a faraway look in her eyes. He watched the sway of her hips as she carried away the dirty dishes. She was cute but she wasn't a patch on the girl he'd seen the night before.

He was just finishing the last sausage, mulling over the taste, wondering what animal it could have come from, aardvark maybe, or smoked ferret, when his mobile rang.

'Summer's dragging,' came a familiar voice.

Chris. His best mate.

'How's things?' Aidan asked.

'I'm meeting Debs later.'

Chris had copped off with the lovely Debs about the same time Aidan got together with Emily. He was always boasting about how far she let him go but Aidan knew he was making it up. Emily told him, and she was a friend of Debs'.

'Hard life,' Aidan said. 'How is Debs?'

'Still hot.'

'You haven't seen Emily around, have you?'

'Pining for her already?'

'No, just wondering, that's all.'

'Don't worry,' said Chris. 'She'll be waiting for you when you get back.'

You'd think I was doing time, Aidan thought. Maybe he was.

'Any idea when you're coming home?' Chris asked. 'There's a lot of stuff to get up to.'

'No, Mum's keeping me in the dark. I'll call you.'

He closed with his best Arnold Schwarzenegger: 'I'll be back.'

Aidan cancelled the call. The young mums and the building workers had gone. The old woman went on sipping her tea, staring in front. Something told him she'd still be there an hour from then. Maybe a year from now there would be a little, old skeleton in Hush Puppies and pearls.

Aidan finished his Coke and left. He'd only been walking for five minutes, moving fast, when he felt beads of sweat on his neck and hairline. It didn't make him that uncomfortable. He liked the way his heart pumped. You don't really get times like this, when most people are either in work or at school and you can wander the streets without a purpose or a care in the world. He could get to like it. He walked as far as a small shopping centre. There was a library, something called a One Stop Shop, and a swimming pool. He pressed his nose to the glass. The pool was a decent size and there were only half a dozen swimmers to get in the way. He decided to make the best of the week before it got packed with kids off school. He was walking back to the dual carriageway when a policeman stopped him.

'Not in school, son?'

'No, I broke up yesterday.'

The policeman wasn't convinced.

'I didn't know the schools had broken up yet. Friday, isn't it?'

Aidan caught his drift.

'I'm not from round here. We broke up on Tuesday.'

'Oh,' he said. 'And where are you from?'

'West Carsley.'

'That on the Wirral?'

'No, Surrey. It's near London.'

The copper gave Aidan an are-you-taking-the-mickey glare.

'I know where Surrey is.'

Aidan wondered why he didn't go catch some real criminals instead of bugging roving teenagers. Always picking on The Yoof.

'So what brings you to Liverpool?'

'My Granddad's ill.'

He took a few details and let Aidan go. Aidan guessed they must be having a truancy drive. That sort of thing was always in the paper, tackling the yob culture, reclaiming the streets. At the top of the road he looked back. The policeman was still watching. Maybe Aidan wasn't so free, after all. His phone went again.

'Guess who?'

'Emily!'

'Missing me?'

'What do you think? I'm bored witless up here.'

'Do you know when you're coming back?'

That again! First Chris, now Emily. He was starting to feel wanted. He'd had such plans for this summer. Lazy, crazy days with Emily before his GCSE year. Why did it all have to go pear-shaped?

'No,' he said. 'Not yet. Look Emily, I'm sorry about all this, seeing as we've only just started going out, and all.'

'Forget it,' she said. 'We've got loads of time.'

Her voice went husky in a way he could get used to.

'I think this is a really good thing you're doing.'

Meaning going to stay with his sick granddad. Emily made him sound like Martin Luther King, Brad Pitt and St Francis of Assisi all rolled up in one wickedly handsome package.

'Granddad's seeing a specialist this week,' he said. 'You've got to make an effort.'

Yes, what a hypocrite.

After a bit of teasing and over-the-airwaves smoochies Aidan cut the connection. The rest of the morning and afternoon he started finding his way around. It wasn't Surrey, that was for sure. The small shopping arcade was run-down, all cracked, peeling paintwork and skipping litter. There was a 50p shop, though some of the bric-a-brac was going for a pound which seemed to infringe the

Trade Descriptions Act. Pensioners trundled shopping trolleys. They waddled by on legs marbled with varicose veins. Like Stilton cheese, Adrian thought. Mums wheeled protesting toddlers, faces pulled tight by the constant whining.

A few yards down the road from the supermarket there was a bus stop. Shiny pebbles of shattered safety glass littered the pavement, a present from the previous evening's drunks. An inspector was waiting. He told Aidan to get a Saveaway ticket. Anywhere in the city off-peak. Aidan found the Pier Head and looked out across the Mersey. Shards of sunlight on the river made it look inviting but he decided to save the ferry trip for another day.

It was ten to four before he got back. He turned the corner into Elmwood Street and there she was, the girl from the night before. She was wearing navy blue school uniform. She was twirling her school tie round her finger. You see most girls in their school uniform and it makes them look like a kid. Not her. She was leaning against a wall, foot on the brickwork, tanned leg bent at the knee. Her head turned slowly and her eyes studied Aidan's face. She was used to being stared at, that much was obvious. That's what made Aidan stare: her confidence. That, and the fact that she was heart-stoppingly gorgeous.

'I'm Aidan,' he said.

'I didn't ask.'

Ouch. He hadn't seen that coming.

'Sorry,' she said, a welcome warmth coming into her brown eyes. 'I come across a bit prickly sometimes.'

Aidan smiled. She was forgiven. With eyes like hers he felt generous.

'I'm staying there,' he told her. 'Number 66. Joe and Mary Kenny's house.'

Her lips curled into a half-smile.

'What's so funny?'

'The way you talk. Where are you from?'

First the copper, now the girl. You'd think he'd just flown in from Siberia. Make a mental note, he told himself: next time you leave home take off the moose antlers.

'West Carsley. It's in Surrey.'

'And where's that?'

He didn't know if she was teasing but he told her anyway.

'Off the M25, orbital nightmare, biggest car park in Western Europe.'

'London?'

'Close.'

He couldn't help peeking at the V of her shirt. She caught him, but she didn't say anything.

'What made you come to this dump?' she asked. 'There must be a lot more to do in London.'

'My Granddad,' he explained. 'He's ill.'

She nodded.

'Yes, I know. He's got that asbestosis, hasn't he?'

Aidan's turn to nod.

'My dad's away on business, so I had no choice but to come along with Mum. Families, eh?'

She took in what he said and changed the subject. He got the impression she didn't want to talk about families.

'Got a girlfriend back in Surrey?' she asked.

A smile played on her lips.

'No,' he lied, hoping he hadn't hesitated too much. 'No girlfriend. You?'

'I don't have a girlfriend in Surrey either,' she deadpanned.

'You know what I mean.'

She pursed her lips. Her eyes were hooded, amused.

'Would you like to do something?' he asked.

17

She sat on the wall and smoothed her skirt over her thighs. He watched. She watched him watching.

'Maybe.'

'Soon?'

'You'll see me around,' she said and walked away. She had some walk. She joined a group of girls who had appeared across the road.

'Ask me again,' she said. 'You never know. You might strike lucky.'

Aidan didn't care that her friends were shrieking with laughter. Strike lucky? He thought he already had.

Three

As he walked through the door Aidan heard voices. It was Mum and Gran.

'He's back! Since when?'

He hesitated, his key still in the lock. There was something about Mum's voice. It was thin, panicky.

'You're sure?' she said. 'You're quite sure?'

Aidan didn't catch Gran's answer.

'Why did he have to come back?' Mum said. 'Why now?'

Aidan closed the front door as quietly as he could and made his way down the hallway on padded feet. Now he heard Granddad's low burr.

'You stay away from him, girl. You've got a family now. You've got a life. It's all water under the bridge.'

Mum's voice snapped back, a whiplash of emotion.

'For God's sake, Dad, what kind of fool do you think I am? I'm not a kid any more. You don't think I'd go within a hundred miles of him if I could help it, do you? You don't have to remind me what he did.'

The conversation stalled. Somebody had registered Aidan's presence. Mum opened the living room door.

'How long have you been standing there?' she demanded.

Her eyes were rimmed with anxiety.

'I just came in,' he told her. 'Who are you talking about?'

She made a ridiculous attempt to wave his question away.

'It's no big deal.'

'You sure?' he asked. 'It sounded pretty big to me.'

He could feel the tension in the room. It was like electricity arcing through the air. Gran looked uncomfortable and slid away into the kitchen. Mum cut his curiosity short.

'Well, it isn't, it's nothing, and you shouldn't eavesdrop.'

She decided to turn defence into attack. 'Where have you been anyway? I was getting worried.'

'I went into the city to take a look at the waterfront.'

Mum nodded.

'What did you think?'

Aidan shrugged.

'It was wet.'

That's me, he thought, always the comedian.

'Sorry,' he said, building bridges. 'It's quite impressive.'

Mum allowed her features to relax into a smile.

'The Maritime Museum's worth a look. Then there's the Tate Modern.'

She realised she'd started sounding like a tourist brochure.

'But you'd rather be out with Chris.'

Correction, Aidan thought, I'd rather be out with Emily. Chris could help fill in the gaps.

'I heard a joke,' Aidan said, 'what do you call a donkey with three legs?'

'A wonky,' Mum said. 'That was going the rounds when I was your age.'

Aidan grinned. Mum grinned back. The joke might be iffy but it was good to smile.

'What did you do for lunch?' she asked.

Granddad pulled a face. Aidan knew why. He called it dinner. Lunch was a Southern invention. Aidan thought about saying he ate it, but that would mean cancelling any Brownie points he had just earned. He decided against it.

'I had a late breakfast. I went over to the supermarket.'

Mum glanced over her shoulder.

'Why didn't you let your gran get you something? You didn't have to hurt her feelings.'

He was about to say sorry, but why bother? It would only cause more grief in the long run. Instead he said:

'She can cook me something now. I'm starving.'

There, he'd finally given the old dear a purpose in life. Forget your husband is dying. Lose yourself in a bacon toastie. Mum grimaced. She didn't think he was funny or clever. Or considerate. He didn't give a toss. He was young, gifted and . . . Well, he was young and gifted.

'What was that, Aidan?' Gran called. 'Are you hungry?'

Good old Gran. Nothing like a bit of her wittering to get Mum off his back.

'Yes, I could eat a whale between two bread factories.'

Gran laughed dutifully and got to work. Aidan crossed the living room and caught Granddad's eye. He held the look. Meaningful stares were the dish of the day.

'How are you doing?' Aidan asked.

It was the best he could do. Granddad had always looked invincible, a rugged, wiry man who descended on Surrey from time to time, casting a disapproving eye over the suburban calm. Too comfortable and complacent for its own good, that was his verdict. The soft South. But he was looking anything but invincible now. The illness seemed to have come from nowhere. One visit, Granddad was fine. The next he was dull and wasted. He seemed to be shrinking. His breathing sounded bad. His cheeks looked hollower than usual.

'I'm OK,' he said, swatting the evidence of his slowly shrivelling body like a troublesome fly. 'Take more than a few asbestos fibres to finish me off. I saw you talking to the Harding girl.'

Aidan's pulse quickened. Brown eyes surfaced in his mind, reaching right into his thoughts, exposing him.

'You know her?'

'Jade. Yes, she was a lovely little girl. She used to play out the front. Always had a smile on her face. Getting a bit hard-faced now though. The company she keeps, poor kid hasn't got a chance.'

Aidan made a mental note of her name, Jade Harding, then glanced out of the window. Granddad had his chair just to the left of it, so he could look out, watch the world go by.

'You must see everything from here,' Aidan said, peering up the street.

'Most things,' Granddad agreed. 'I don't have much else to do with my time, not since my lungs got worse.'

He thumped his chest, which seemed like a bad idea.

'Going out isn't really an option,' he said. 'I'm always breathless. I feel such an idiot, having to hold on to somebody's gate while I get my breath. Illness and old age. Sodding nuisances, the pair of them. Stop you doing anything.'

'There's always the TV,' Aidan said.

'Never anything on,' said Granddad with a derisive snort. 'I may be ill but I'm not a vegetable. You won't see me glued to daytime TV like some dole-ite. I read a bit. I watch the goings-on.'

The way he said it, Aidan realised there were a lot of goings-on in Elmwood Street.

'It must be bad news, living like this.'

Granddad nodded and caught Mum's eye.

'There's worse things.'

Aidan didn't know if that was directed at him or at her. Granddad could be pretty cryptic. Either way, it didn't make much sense. Sense would come later. When the conversation ran dry Aidan sat down in an armchair and watched TV. It was *Countdown*. Whenever he was home in time Dad would sit glued to the screen, scribbling the numbers and letters down in a notebook. If he beat the contestants he was like a cat that had OD'd on the cream. If he didn't he had a face like a smacked behind. He was a big kid, Dad. Aidan glanced at the screen.

'Seven,' he said, feeling very pleased with himself. 'Rations.'

It sounded good for seven points. Eat your heart out, Dad.

'Nine,' said Granddad. 'Relations.'

'Where'd you get that from?' Aidan asked.

Granddad tapped his forehead.

'I might not have a fancy education,' he said, 'but I'm not daft.'

He certainly wasn't. Aidan tried harder after that but Granddad seemed to have lost interest. He didn't want a competition, which was frustrating. Aidan was competitive in everything he did, in his schoolwork, in sport. He only got really interested in Emily when he caught Chris watching her and realised she was the biggest catch in the school. The moment Aidan expressed an interest Chris just moved over. The main reason he was Aidan's best mate is he knew who was number one.

Dad called just as the family were sitting down for tea. He asked after Granddad and made some small talk. Then he told Aidan about Singapore: the food, the hotel, what movies you could get on cable, stuff like that. He told a few lame jokes as usual. Aidan told some back. As usual.

He even told the three-legged donkey but Dad had heard it too. When Aidan put the phone down he was smiling. So he was going to be up here a few days, big deal. It was an interesting city and there was always Jade. Life was still good, nothing out of the ordinary.

Or so he thought.

After tea Aidan went out looking for Jade. He saw her crossing the waste ground at the bottom of the street where a speed-bumped road led to the dual carriageway. That was the story of Elmwood: a pub at one end, a dual carriageway at the other, and boredom in between. Jade had changed out of her uniform. She was wearing a white, sleeveless top, a short, mustard-coloured skirt and flip flops.

'Jade. Hey, Jade. Hold up.'

He jogged over to her. She frowned.

'How'd you get my name?'

'A little bird told me.'

She laughed.

'A nosy old bird, you mean. Your Granddad's been at that window again, then?'

'Yes,' he said. 'It's about all he's got to pass the time.'

'I couldn't handle it,' Jade said. 'Living like that, being eaten away.'

She shuddered.

'I'd rather be dead.'

Aidan didn't have an answer.

'Are you doing anything this evening?' he asked.

'Same as usual,' she said. 'Hanging round.'

'Is that all you do?' he asked. He didn't see that much difference between her hanging round the streets and Granddad sitting at his window. 'Don't you ever go any-where?'

'Such as?'

'I don't know. Swimming? Cinema? I'm always going to the movies with my mates. We live down the multiplex.'

He was careful to leave Emily out of the equation.

'We do a Film Club at school, all the oldies, the classics.'

He was feeling pretty pleased with himself. King Aidan the Interesting, but Jade wrinkled her nose.

'That sounds fun,' she said sarcastically.

'You don't mean that, do you?' he said, more than a bit put out.

She laughed.

'Of course not.'

'What's wrong with a Film Club?'

She mooned her eyes.

'I bet you're a right nerd on the quiet,' she said, nudging him playfully.

He liked the little nudge but he didn't like being called a nerd. Nerd! OK, he was academic but he was captain of the swimming team too, a Hunk. No buck teeth and milk bottle glasses for him. For a moment or two he was completely wrong-footed. He squirmed out a reply. This wasn't the kind of territory he wanted to explore.

'Why'd you say that?'

'It's the way you sound. I can read boys like a book.'

'Go on then,' he said. 'Read me. I dare you.'

Jade gave him her knowing smile. The way she poked fun was gentle really, but he felt as if those dark eyes were peering right into his soul.

'You help in the school library . . .'

His heart yelped. How the hell did she know that?

'You've read *Lord of the Rings* twice.'

Wha—? His vote in the Big Read! And there was more to come.

'You love *The Simpsons* but not the last two series. Your

favourite film is *The Matrix* or, hang on, what's it called, *Citizen Kane*.'

Who was this girl?

'The nerds all love *Citizen Kane*, even though it was made six million years before they were born.'

She mimicked a film buff.

'Ooh, those revolutionary camera angles.'

She gave a mischievous smile.

'Let's see . . . Yes, you listen to Coldplay compilations. You keep tropical fish.' He must have stiffened visibly because she laughed out loud. It was a rich, warm sound. It made him want to laugh along. There was another sound too, the noise of preconceptions crashing to the floor. Jade had an intelligence that was sharp as a scalpel, and he'd just been dissected. Served him right for underestimating her.

'You're wrong about *Lord of the Rings*,' he said. 'I've only read it once. And there's no fish. It's an iguana.'

Chris was baby-sitting Iggy round his house. That's Chris's house, not Iggy's. Iguanas aren't big on house-ownership. Jade looked at Aidan sideways.

'What about the rest of it?'

His silence told her all she needed to know. Just two days before Aidan left home he and Chris had counted the *Citizen Kane* references in *The Simpsons*. Jade clapped her hands with glee.

'Gotcha!' she squealed, just like a little kid. 'Gotcha down to a tee.'

'Oh, quit gloating,' he said.

Jade pulled tongues. She was really enjoying her little victory.

'How did you do that anyway?' he asked.

'Easy,' she said. 'I know boys. I know the hard lads; I know the saddos.'

'You know your films too,' he said.

'Didn't say I didn't,' she retorted. 'But we were talking about you.'

She nudged him. He did like that playful nudge.

'You know, I've even met one or two like you.'

Phew, not a saddo then!

'You think you're pretty clever, don't you?' he said.

'I know I am,' Jade said, by way of correction.

Aidan looked around and pointed out a lad two, maybe three years older than them. The smile vanished from Jade's face. Aidan threw out his challenge.

'Read him.'

Her eyes shifted.

'It isn't worth the trouble.'

Their interest must have been noticed because he came over.

'I haven't seen you around before,' he said.

The strong Scouse accent bordered on caricature.

'I'm Aidan Shaw,' Aidan told him. 'I'm staying at number 66.'

He could sense Jade almost shrinking beside him. He wasn't imagining it.

'The Kennys?' the older boy said, interest flaring in his eyes.

Aidan nodded.

'They're my grandparents.'

'I'm Paul,' he said. 'Paul Gorman.'

He showed lots of white teeth but it wasn't what you'd really call a smile. It was just for show. At that moment Aidan realised he wasn't going to like Paul Gorman. Maybe it was because of Jade's reaction. She seemed hostile, but there was something else. They had history.

'Is Jade keeping you entertained?' he asked.

Aidan didn't like his choice of words. Everything Paul said seemed loaded. Nor did he like the way Paul had moved close to her. Jade wouldn't meet his eyes. She was looking really uncomfortable.

'We just met,' Aidan said, conscious of a slight wobble in his voice.

Paul showed his even, white teeth. His mouth smiled. His eyes didn't. They were dead. He could have kept Iggy company.

'Everybody likes Jade,' he said.

She kept looking down. She didn't look up until he'd walked away whistling. Aidan watched him go. He had a tattooed band of blue-black thorns circling his right bicep and a gold ring pierced his left eyebrow. He was tall, wiry, looked like he could handle himself. He could handle me, Aidan decided, that was for certain. Aidan had always been sporty but he was no fighter.

'What was that about?' he asked.

'Nothing,' Jade said, still uncomfortable. 'He fancies himself, that's all.'

A voice came into Aidan's head:

And what about you, Jade?

Great, he thought, second day here and he was jealous already. Given he was doing the dirty on Emily, it was a bit rich. He wanted to let loose a stream of questions. He didn't. Paul had joined a knot of lads on the street corner. They shouted a few things in Aidan's direction. He couldn't make them out. Something to do with the accent, he supposed. Jade wrapped her arms round herself. Aidan decided to change the subject.

'Come swimming with me.'

'What?'

'You heard.'

'You're full of yourself,' she said.

'That's right. I'm a good swimmer too. So are you coming?'

28

Her gaze flicked to the group on the corner but when her eyes met Aidan's the shadows drained out of them.

'OK,' she said, brushing her hair away. 'You're on.'

They hung around for a couple of hours, talking, laughing, just being together. Jade's friends joined them for a while then drifted off, leaving them to their verbal duel. Most of the time Aidan lost, but he didn't care. She liked being with him, it was obvious, and he certainly liked being with her. From time to time Jade would say things that broke the spell. It was as though she couldn't handle anything that was, well, nice. Aidan had a feeling this was a girl who came equipped with her own self-destruct button. But as night came and long shadows bled down the city streets he felt so close to her. It was after eleven when he went in, the sounds of the street in his head, the smell of Jade's hair and perfume in his nostrils.

Before he closed the door, he glanced back hoping to catch a last glimpse of her. A sapphire blue BMW coasted down the street, slowing down as it passed his grandparents' house. Electric windows purred open. The driver and passenger turned in his direction. They seemed to hold his gaze and Aidan felt a distinct prickle of unease. For a brief moment time seemed to stand still, then the car picked up speed and turned at the top of the street. The crescent moon hung like a cold, thin smile over the city glow.

The Gunslinger

His eyes follow the words the way a reptile's follow a
fly. They devour. They consume the terrors held in
the book's pages. Nobody would have him down for
a reader. They would look at his stocky frame, his
dull, unsmiling eyes and assume he doesn't have an
idea in his head. But they would be wrong. He thinks.
He strips meaning from an epic quest. He lives the
black dreams of a haunted wasteland. He wanders
roads of desolation. He doesn't read widely. One
writer fills his imagination; Stephen King. One man's
vision stokes the fires of his dreams with all the fuel
they need. A dark tower rises in the distance. The
Gunslinger will reach it one day. There he will crucify
a man who has been his closest friend since boy-
hood. He will do it because it needs to be done. He
has no qualms about it. It is his destiny. The friend's
dying will be his becoming.

Four

Next morning Aidan was up before eight o'clock. The sun had risen before him. It was hot. When he went downstairs Gran was sitting at the kitchen table cradling a mug of tea, the sunlight on her face. There was no sign of Mum or Granddad.

'Where is everybody?' he asked.

Gran started as though a ghost had walked through her.

'Aidan!'

Her fingers fluttered in front of her face.

'You gave me such a fright. I was in a daydream.'

She composed herself for a moment or two then suddenly bolted out of her seat.

'I'll make you a cooked breakfast. It'll be much better than that supermarket.'

She wasn't going to forget that in a hurry.

'My bacon won't have stood in its own fat half the morning like theirs.'

'Just toast please, Gran,' Aidan said.

She went to protest but he held up his hand.

'Honestly,' he said. 'It's all I want. I'm going swimming. I don't want anything too heavy. You'd have me sinking right to the bottom. Toast. One slice.'

He listened for movement around the house.

'Isn't Mum up?'

'She went out about ten minutes ago.'

Aidan glanced at his watch. Two minutes to eight.

'What? At this time?'

'She's got some messages to run.'

Messages. Scouse slang for errands.

'Messages? What messages? Who does she know round here after all this time?'

Gran glanced at him then her eyes slid away. He'd touched a nerve but didn't know how.

'Here's your toast,' she said. 'Do you want jam or marmalade?'

'Toast will do fine,' he told her. 'Just a smear of butter.'

Breakfast had lost its attraction. He had an acidy grumble of anxiety in his gut. There was no focus to it. He couldn't hook it onto anything in particular but there it was, real as the scarring on Granddad's lungs, a black hole at the heart of the house.

'How is Granddad?' Aidan said. 'Really.'

'You know about the asbestos, don't you?'

He nodded.

'Yes, Granddad kind of told me about it.'

'Kind of?'

'You know what he's like, tight-lipped. He doesn't give much away.'

Gran nodded. She looked worn out.

'He worked with the stuff for years,' she said. 'Nobody told you about the dangers then. Do you know, I had it on my ironing board for years, just flaking away. It's a wonder I'm not riddled with it too. Joe can remember him and the other fellows larking about, using it to play snowballs. It was white, you see. They used to ball it up in their hands and throw it around. They didn't know what it was going to do to their health. Two of the old gang are dead,

Gerard Mooney three years ago, Jimmy Kavanagh earlier this year. The little fibres cut your lungs to shreds. When Joe went for his check-up he found out that it had taken a turn for the worse.'

'Cancer?'

Gran nodded.

'Oh, we've known that for weeks.'

Aidan flinched. This was worse than preferring a supermarket breakfast to hers. Mum had made a point of telling him about the cancer, warning him to be careful what he said. He'd allowed it to slip from his mind, as if it didn't matter.

'Now it's spreading. He's such a good man, Aidan love. Some fellows, they used to give their wives pocket money and keep the rest, spend it in the boozer or down the bookies. They treated women like little kids or skivvies, not partners for life. Not my Joe. He would always come in on a Friday and leave his pay packet on the kitchen table. If we were saving for something, he would tell his mates he wouldn't be down the club.'

Aidan understood the anguish. You die in a car accident, it's sudden, final. You go through a long illness, the grieving begins while you're still alive. You get to hear your own obituaries.

'The girls and I always came first,' Gran said.

Her eyes were welling with tears. She laughed through the pain.

'Why Joe?' she said. 'Why's it always the good ones . . . ?'

She stammered brokenly and went out of the room. Aidan could see her in the hallway, wiping her eyes. Her shoulders were heaving. He wanted to say something. He didn't. He wasn't good at that sort of thing. Who is at fifteen? Finally, she returned.

'You must think I'm a stupid old woman,' she said.

He wanted to comfort her. He really did. He just didn't know how.

'Of course I don't think that,' was all he could manage. 'Anyway, sixty isn't old these days.'

He mightn't have paid much attention to Mum's medical updates but at least he'd remembered Gran's age, within a couple of years anyway.

'Charmer,' she said, still mopping her eyes.

'Look, I'd better get off. If I leave it much longer the pool will be packed.'

It wasn't true. The local schools weren't breaking up until that afternoon. He'd have all the room he wanted.

He didn't go straight to the pool. He waited around for Jade, watching the breeze whipping round the litter of Styrofoam cups and crisp packets. At twenty to nine she came out of her front door. He was about to say something when he saw her turn on her heel and shout back at somebody indoors.

'Problems?' he said.

For a moment she looked past him. Then she shook her head.

'Only my stupid bitch of a mother.'

Not for the first time, Jade shocked him to silence.

'What's with you?' she said, seeing his face.

'You just called your mum a bitch.'

Her eyes flashed. Was she crying?

'So? That's what she is.'

Her voice sounded thick, all right. She was obviously upset. It didn't stop her turning and screaming the word again at the window where a woman's face had appeared. This older woman had the same dark hair as Jade, but there the similarity ended. Aidan guessed that she must be in her mid-thirties. She looked ten years older. Her hair was scraped back from her face which, like Jade's, was a sun bed bronze. Jade's mum screamed something but the words bounced back off the windows. Still, Aidan got the message. Most of north Liverpool did. They were halfway down the road before Jade looked at him.

'Have you been waiting for me?' she said.

'Sort of.'

With Aidan everything was 'kind of' or 'sort of'. His way of sounding off-hand and cool. Jade let herself press against him for a moment. He liked the softness and the warmth. He allowed his face to come close to her hair, smelling the faintest trace of perfume. For a moment he thought they were going to kiss, then she pulled away again.

'So have you been waiting?'

Aidan grinned sheepishly.

'OK, I have. There's no law against it, is there?'

'Forget about me,' Jade said, wiping her eyes. 'Don't waste your time. I'm bad news. Stick with your nice girlfriend back in Surrey.'

He recoiled in mock horror, or wounded innocence, or whatever act he was trying to put on.

'I don't have a girlfriend,' he protested.

Jade's face twisted. It was obvious she was still wound up over the row with her mum. But there was something else: disappointment in him.

'Oh, pull the other one,' she snapped. 'It's got sleigh bells. What do you think I am, thick or something?'

He tried to carry on the protest. Jade wasn't interested.

'Save your stories for Nancy Normal,' she said.

OK, deep breath. It was confession time.

'Her name's Emily.'

There, he'd told the truth. Jade shrugged.

'Whatever.'

Something in her voice broke and died. They reached the bus stop. He felt like a baby who'd had its dummy snatched.

'Does this mean you won't be going swimming with me tonight?'

That whine he hated so much had crept into his voice. Jade screwed her face into an expression that was part grimace, part smile. A civil war was going on inside her.

'No,' she said finally, her voice dropping almost to a whisper. 'Whatever gave you that idea?'

'I thought . . .'

She started talking fast. It was pretty obvious, even to him, that it was all an act.

'Well, you thought wrong,' she said. 'You want to mess this Emily around, that's your business. It's no skin off my nose. It's not like we're the big Romeo and Juliet deal. It's a laugh.'

He wanted to contradict her, tell her it was a big deal. It certainly felt that way. In the end he didn't say much at all. He was just relieved she hadn't dumped him.

'So we've got a date?'

Jade joined the friends who were waiting at the bus stop and started jostling aboard the bus. The tears were all gone, her streetwise mask was back. She gave him a mischievous finger wave. Soon the whole group were blowing kisses and laughing. God, girls were scary in a group!

He watched the bus pull round the corner. By the time it had gone most of the conversation was already history. He punched the air.

He had a date all right.

There were cobwebs in the hedges on the way to the pool. They were hung with dew and sparkled like fine necklaces.

Aidan shook a sprig of privet and made the dewdrops dance. Then he saw the fly. It was struggling in the heart of the web, its fragile legs pedalling pathetically. The movement made the web bounce and shudder. It was still struggling when the spider appeared. He watched the predator coming closer. Suddenly the warm feelings left by his chat with Jade vanished. Seeing the spider moving along the web made a fat, slimy slug of nausea twist in his gut. Before it could strike he ripped the web apart and walked away.

He was angry and he wasn't sure why.

When he arrived home from the pool, Mum was back. She started with small talk. Aidan paid little attention.

'Who did you go to see?' he asked.

He didn't really know why it mattered, but it did. Back in Surrey Mum was utterly predictable. Here, in these new surroundings, this city where she had grown up, Aidan realised there were other dimensions to her. Somehow that was unsettling.

'An old school friend,' Mum said. 'You wouldn't know her.'

Too easy. Too pat. Aidan hit her with a question.

'What's her name?'

Mum's eyes widened.

'What is this, the Spanish Inquisition?'

'I asked her name, that's all.'

There was a light in Mum's eyes, a warning fire. It told him, whatever game you're playing, I'm walking off the pitch.

'Are you calling me a liar?' she said. 'Here.'

She handed him the cordless phone.

'Her name's Carol Flaherty if you must know. Do you want the number?'

37

Aidan shoved the handset back at her. She took it and met him eyeball to eyeball, wagging the phone. It made a change from her finger.

'Don't you ever try to interrogate me again,' she said.

Over the top, he thought, *way* over the top. He wanted to ask her: why at eight o'clock in the morning? And why so soon after all the subterfuge the night before? He did neither, though he did wonder what she would have done if he'd tried to phone this Carol. Mum had been on edge ever since they left home, and it wasn't just about Grand-dad's health either. If he was the point of this trip, what was she doing vanishing at the crack of dawn, leaving him to his own devices? Either you're snapping my head off, Aidan thought, or you're silent, withdrawn in your own little world. He'd never seen her so brittle, or so caught up in her own affairs. And here's a priceless piece of advice for all teenagers. When the floor you're standing on is made of glass and it's starting to crack, don't start stamping. Aidan decided to let it go. Mum took a deep breath then spoke again, more quietly this time.

'Your dad phoned again. You missed him.'

'What did he say?'

'The hotel is nice. He was just on his way out to a meeting.'

'He's homesick, isn't he?'

Mum snapped a bobble round her hair.

'Mark's always been a home boy.'

There was warmth in her voice. She loved that about him, his reliability. Not like some men, she would say darkly. But what did she know about *some men*?

'I'm driving your Granddad up to the hospital to see the consultant,' she said, dangling her car keys from her index finger. 'Gran's going with us. What are you planning to do with yourself?'

38

'I was thinking of getting one of those Saveaway tickets again, take a look round.'

Mum nodded and pulled a couple of tenners out of her purse.

'Here.'

'I've got money.'

Mum shoved the notes into his hand. In some strange way he felt as though he was being bought.

'Now you've got more. Just try to be back for your tea.'

'Sure,' he said. 'No problem.'

Liverpool is a city of ghosts, of echoes. It feels as if half the population has gone in a couple of generations. When you gaze out across the Mersey there are many Liverpools moving in the mist. There is the Liverpool of Empire: sugar, tobacco and slavery. Then there is the Liverpool of gentrified flats and heritage trails; of the Beatles and the Cavern and the Liver birds; of Gerry and the Pacemakers and that timeless ferry.

Most of all there is the Liverpool of loss: ruined cityscapes disintegrating under the grey clouds and the afterimages of all the people who have left to look for a better life. A good example of that is a boarded up pub called the Overhead Railway at the far end of Elmwood Street. The overhead railway, after which it was named, once ran the length of the dockland. No longer economic, it was torn down years ago. Now the pub is going the same way. Half the day kids pound their football against its walls.

The brickwork is tagged with their names. People still live on the top floor. At night the electric lights illuminate the security boards.

Aidan wasn't interested in history though. All he cared about was Jade and being fifteen and having some fun. But lives leave trails like tripwires. He didn't know it but he was already starting to stumble over them.

Most of the day he wandered round the heart of the city, looking at trainers in JJB Sports, exploring the Liverpool FC shop and stopping off for a burger at the McDonald's in St John's Precinct. It was his second trip and he was beginning to find his way round. He walked as far as Hope Street, which joins the two cathedrals. He stood a while looking at the Metropolitan cathedral – Paddy's Wigwam as it's known – then continued up to the Anglican. He watched its head-and-shoulders shape looming closer. It was hot.

He was still looking round when a thought occurred to him. This was the longest he had ever stayed with his grandparents. Come to think of it, they had always come down to Surrey to visit. He went back in his mind, trying to think of one time he had slept over. He couldn't think of a single occasion. There had only ever been flying visits, and not so many of them. Suddenly a worm of curiosity was twisting in his mind.

At seven o'clock that evening he plunged into the swimming pool for the second time. On this occasion Jade was with him. It beat ploughing up and down on his own. The white swimming costume she was wearing made him realise she had to be using a sun bed at least a couple of times a week. What else could explain that healthy Chernobyl glow?

He found it hard to argue with Gran's reaction when she found out who he was hanging round with.

'The Harding girl,' she'd said, disappointed. 'Oh Aidan, that fake suntan. She's virtually orange!'

'Aren't you supposed to be sixteen?' he asked Jade.

'What?'

'Before you use a sun bed.'

Jade shrugged and slid into the water, cupping her arms round the tops of her arms the way skinny little kids do.

'It's freezing,' she said.

'Don't be such a wimp,' he told her. 'It's 84 degrees. So what about the sun bed?'

'What are you?' she asked, brown eyes flashing 'My mum? We've got a sun bed in the house. So what? All the girls go on them.'

'Yes, but what about the dangers?'

He heard himself repeating all the stuff Mum had told him, how you'd end up like a brown prune and get skin cancer. Doctor Aidan. But he couldn't stop.

'Aren't you worried you'll damage your skin?'

'Oh, stop going on,' she said. 'You're a right old woman sometimes. I thought we were going to have a laugh. Anyway, it's not like you're going to be around to see what I turn out like.'

He ached to reassure her. He wanted to put his finger to her lips and tell her he'd be there for her. He didn't. It would have sounded ridiculous. She knew about Emily and that didn't exactly make him God's gift to fidelity.

'You never know,' he said, snaking an arm round her waist underwater.

She pulled away.

'Listen,' she said, her eyes suddenly hard. 'So long as you're here we can go out, have a bit of fun. But that's it. Don't go making any stupid promises. A few days and you'll be gone. I won't see you again. Now cut the crap and let's enjoy this for what it is.' Jade was always full of surprises. A little kid shuddering by the pool one minute, Miss Streetwise the next. He found it unsettling. He wanted to ask what she thought it was they had. In the circumstances it would have been a bad idea.

'Show me your strokes,' she said.

He put his arm round her again and wriggled his fingers against her ribs.

'Not that sort,' she giggled. 'Let me see you swim.'

He did a length of crawl.

'You're good,' she said, clearly impressed. 'Can you do that hard one?'

'Butterfly?'

'Yes, that's the one.'

He ploughed down the pool and back. He did a tumble turn, just to show off.

'Are you double-jointed or something?' she asked, staring at his shoulders.

Aidan shook his head.

'It just comes with practice. Come on, you haven't even moved out of the shallow end yet.'

He splashed her with water. She came back at him flailing and laughing. They were getting a disapproving look from the lifeguard but neither of them cared. Aidan felt her against him. He felt the flutter of her heartbeat against his chest and his body surged. He didn't want his time with her to end. He was just so completely alive.

They didn't go straight home after their swim. They hung around, talked, had pizza. They held hands all the way back but when they passed the Overhead Railway pub and Jade saw the top of Elmwood Street she slid her fingers out of his.

'Something wrong?' he said. 'Don't you want to be seen with me?'

He tried to keep his voice even and his eyes gentle. He didn't think he was very convincing. Jade frowned but she didn't answer. The furrowed brow was all he was getting. Half the lights were on down the twilit street as they

parted. The rest were just beginning to stutter to life as if
the dusk had become too heavy a burden to shrug off. The
streets were still. But, like the black waters of the river,
they were deceptive.

Under the surface there were predators.

'I had a good time,' Jade said as they turned into Elmwood.

She started to walk away.

'Where are you going?' he asked.

'I'm just going to see my friends before I go in.'

'And that's it?'

She stopped and looked back.

'What were you expecting?'

He didn't know. He watched her cross the road and felt
suddenly empty. Figures moved under the streetlamps,
their voices carrying in the night. One of them was Paul
Gorman. He started towards Aidan then thought better of
it. Aidan was still wondering why when he heard a voice.

'You're the lad staying at number 66, aren't you?'

Aidan looked round. A man had stepped out of the
shadows. He was wearing black trousers and a black
tee-shirt, with only a gold chain to offset the effect. His
shoes looked expensive. He looked cheap. The man in
black. How corny was that?

'Are you staying with the Kennys?' he said.

He had a strong Scouse accent and there was a twist of
laughter in his voice. He found something funny, which is
more than Aidan did. Aidan looked down at the pavement
and went to move past the stranger. That's when he saw
the blue BMW. The driver was watching their conversation with a bored expression. Paul was just up the
road, his attention flicking from the car to Aidan and the
man in black. Aidan wondered why he was so interested.
He opted for boldness.

'Look,' Aidan said, trying to hide the shake in his voice. 'I don't know you.'

The man wasn't that tall, average height really, but he gave Aidan the impression of power. He looked as if he worked out. His arms and neck were thick. His eyes were points of darkness in his fleshy face. He watched Aidan go. As Aidan reached the front door he looked round. The man in black had got in the passenger seat of the blue BMW.

'No,' he said. 'You don't know me, but I know you.'

The way he said it, the knowing look in his eyes, struck deep. Night invaded Aidan. Rivulets of darkness trickled into every atom of his being.

The Gunslinger

He opens his book and reads. He holds the book carefully, almost reverently. He doesn't bend it back the way some people do. That breaks the spine and you don't do that to a book. You don't do that to a story that sums you up better than you could yourself. He reads a couple of pages then looks along the street. The offer will come any day now. It is only a matter of time. They need to get their man, he thinks, but they will have to get past me first. They're not sure they can do that. So they will buy me, or try to, and I won't come cheap. He smiles and starts reading again. No, I won't come cheap at all.

Five

Aidan stood for some time in the hallway of his grand-parents' house. The small, dark eyes seemed to float before him. The flat, insinuating voice seeped through his mind. His heart was banging. It was only when Gran called to see if it was him that he stepped away from the front door. He was still on edge after the encounter in the street outside. Out there, in the warm, dark night something was happening, something that would pick up speed and eventually carry him away. He wanted to call a halt to the currents that were swirling around him. He felt like a straw being borne away on rushing waters.

His mind was racing, trying to make sense of these stray episodes. He had a vague understanding that he was a piece of a jigsaw puzzle being put together around him. No story is the tale of just one person. While he was crawling into bed half an hour later, a man who was also part of the puzzle was taking a phone call.

About the time Aidan was looking up at the ceiling wondering what to make of his meeting with BMW man, the Gunslinger was popping his car alarm and watching the lights flash. He chuckled. Why bother with the alarm at all? He knew all the car thieves in his neighbourhood and they would have chewed their own right legs off rather than touch his motor. They knew what was good for them, and he wasn't. He was the darkest corner of their worst nightmare.

He let himself in the house, shouted something to his wife who was already in bed and went into the kitchen to get something to eat. He sat at the kitchen table munching a duck wrap from Marks and Spencers. He liked M&S, whatever the trendies said. His mother shopped there when she had the money, which meant when he handed her a roll of the folding stuff. Only the best for the best, she used to say, you can swear by Marksies. She always took the wad without a single question about where he got it. Trust. He liked that. No fuss, no complication. She was the only one who never asked stupid questions, his old girl. He smiled. She was good to him. Still smiling, he picked up *The Dark Tower: The Gunslinger* by Stephen King and read the first line, about a man in black fleeing across the desert. How many times had he read it, five, six? However many it was, it would have a new-found significance by the end of that night.

Most people identify with a book's hero. Not the Gunslinger. He wasn't the kid stumbling through the sewers in search of the beast. He was the beast. He wasn't the woman and child scrambling through the bathroom window. He was the axe man coming through the door. He wasn't the band of brothers pledging eternal friendship. He was the taunting clown who teased his terrified victims. But the Gunslinger's weapon wasn't fangs, or an axe. It was his firearm. He knew that the gun is the true image of the modern age. It knows the price of life the way nothing else does, that it is gone in an instant, gone and lost forever. And when the gun has done its work and silence returns to the streets they belong to the strong. The Gunslinger was finishing his aromatic duck when his mobile rang.

'Yes?'

He listened. It was the offer he'd been expecting.

'Double the money,' he said, 'and you've got a deal.'

He listened to the silence at the other end of the phone. This was a game he was always going to win. He knew the buyer would pay the price. It took a few moments but the buyer finally agreed.

'Half tomorrow,' he said. 'Half when it's done.'

The buyer tried to bargain.

'I'm not haggling over the price,' said the Gunslinger. 'It's non-negotiable. You know you can't do it without me. If I don't help you it doesn't happen.'

The buyer caved as the Gunslinger knew he would.

'Good doing business with you,' he said.

The Gunslinger ended the call. He thought about trust and betrayal and shrugged his shoulders.

'Money for old rope,' he said.

Six

Midway through Saturday afternoon Aidan noticed that the street was coming alive outside. School was out and the summer holidays had begun. Thoughts of the BMW and the man in black had started to evaporate. Aidan had lived his life too long in the comfort zone to be wrenched free of his usual complacency. Maybe he was deluding himself, but he put it all down to a simple idea: the crazies come out at night. Now that the sun was up and the crazies were all indoors, he was more interested in whether Jade would be appearing. He craned his neck to look up the street. There were knots of lads on the corners shoving one another and laughing a bit too loud for it to be anything but show. Girls were parading up and down, trying to catch their eye without looking too interested. They were all out of school uniform. Carnival time. The half dozen girls closest to the window were wearing their lightweight summer outfits: sleeveless and all but backless. It looked as though they had dressed for the heavy mid-afternoon heat. Aidan went to the front door. He was looking around for Jade when Paul Gorman approached.

'Why didn't you tell me who you were?' he said.

Aidan must have frowned because Paul chuckled.

'Oh sure, like you don't know what I'm talking about.'

He shook his head and started to walk away.

'You crack me up, you really do. Still, you and Deegan. I'd never have put you together.'

Aidan stared after him for a moment.

'Deegan?' he said.

Paul repeated his humourless chuckle.

'Yes, Deegan. Surely you haven't forgotten.'

Aidan was still puzzling over their conversation when he saw Jade.

'Hi,' he said, 'I've been waiting for you.'

She put on a yawn. Cosmetic, he decided. For his benefit. It was to show she wasn't all that interested. He didn't believe her.

'Well,' she said, dropping the pretence of superiority. 'Here I am.'

There she was. She was wearing a white halter-neck top and white shorts. She liked white. He was no fan of the sun bed tan, but he had to admit she looked good. Radiant was the word. She was sitting on a garden wall. When she crossed her legs her top knee shone. He noticed these things.

'Does this make you a free agent?' he asked.

She gave him a mischievous, sideways glance.

'I suppose.'

OK, he thought, here goes nothing.

'So what are we doing with the rest of the day?'

As if Emily didn't exist.

'Full of yourself, aren't you?' said Jade.

'I've a lot to be full of myself about,' he answered.

It wasn't great grammar but she smiled.

'Where are you taking me?' she asked.

He liked the sound of that. Taking her.

'The Albert Dock's all right,' he said.

Jade wrinkled her nose.

'They took us there on a school trip,' she said. 'When I was eight.'

'This isn't a school trip,' he reminded her. 'And, just in case you hadn't noticed, you're all grown up.'

She smiled again. He'd said the right thing. Twice. He was on a roll.

'Come in ours,' she said. 'I'm going to get some money.'

'I'll see you in there,' he said. 'Got to tell Mum where I'm going.'

'Run along then,' said Jade.

Like a good little boy. Didn't she just love these barbed one-liners. He must have blushed. She was making fun of him. He was back in a couple of minutes.

'Jade,' he shouted through the open front door.

She told him to come in. The moment he stepped indoors he decided it was a mistake. The hall carpet was thick with cat hair. It didn't look as though it had been vacuumed in months. There were even a few crushed cigarette ends. The stair carpet was the same. The whole hallway was dingy and in need of a clean. The wallpaper had peeled away completely in places. There was a musty smell, part cat, part decay. He finally found Jade in the living room. She noticed the way he was looking round the place and her voice faltered. She was used to the mess and he was reminding her how it looked to outsiders. Suddenly she was seeing it through somebody else's eyes and her humiliation was obvious.

'I shouldn't have asked you in, should I?' she said.

When he hesitated, she laughed.

'It's OK,' she said. 'No need to pretend. You can say it. It's Slum City, isn't it?'

She bit her lip, a hurt little girl, then the hardness came back. With Jade, it never stayed away long. Aidan's problem was knowing which version he was dealing with at any one time.

'The dirty cow never cleans,' she said.

Hard version, obviously.

Aidan didn't ask whether Jade cleaned. The living room was worse than the hall. There were a couple of empty vodka bottles lying on their side by a greasy-looking armchair. There was a strong smell of cigarette smoke on account of the unemptied ashtrays.

'Now you know why I talk about Mum the way I do,' Jade said. 'She's just a sad old slapper who can't keep herself together.'

Aidan wasn't completely convinced by the tough act. Jade loved her mum. It wept out of the pain in her voice. That's why it bothered her the way the house was. He glanced at the vodka bottles.

'Those hers?'

Jade nodded.

'She spends most of her money on booze and ciggies. Most days she doesn't get out of bed until midday. I've been getting myself up for school since I was in juniors. No way could I rely on her to do it. She's got every addiction going.'

She picked up a medicine bottle. With a hollow laugh, she gave it a rattle.

'She smokes, she drinks, she pops pills.'

She gave the biggest grimace yet.

'She can't do without men either. That's the biggest craving of the lot. There's a new one every week and they're losers, every last one of them.'

She shook her head as if reliving a nasty experience. Her eyes flashed, half an inch from tears.

'You want to know the worst thing, a couple of them have come on to me. She didn't even notice. Too drunk. Too desperate.'

It was Aidan's turn to grimace. He tried to imagine living like that. Back home he had stability in truckloads. A major crisis was when he dropped a few per cent in an exam or Dad missed a sales target. Mum didn't have crises. She was their rock, always there. She was a shoulder for her boys to cry on. Aidan couldn't get a handle on Jade's life.

'Come on,' Jade said, giving the place a last dismissive once-over. 'Let's get out of here.'

He didn't need telling twice.

The Albert Dock, with its colonnades, shops and coach loads of sightseers, is Liverpool looking on the bright side. They stood slightly apart from the tourist bustle, looking out across the river.

'Do you want to take the ferry?' Aidan said.

'Done it,' Jade said. 'I told you, when I was eight.'

'That's seven years ago,' I said. 'And you weren't with me then. Besides, I haven't done it. Humour me.'

He winked and added:

'Please.'

Jade shrugged and they walked over to the office at the Pier Head. Moments later they were walking down to the landing stage.

'Do you know somebody called Deegan?' he asked.

'Deegan?'

Jade was searching her memory banks.

'I have heard it,' she said. 'There's . . .'

Just for a second, her eyes widened. Aidan thought she had something for him. He was in for a disappointment.

'No,' she said, shaking her head. 'I don't remember.'

A look passed between them.

'Why do you want to know?' she asked.

He told her about Paul Gorman.

'Can you find out for me?' he asked. 'It can't be that hard, not if he's local.'

'OK,' she said. 'I'll try. But, listen Aidan, if Paul knows this man, you'd better forget about him. Paul's no good.'

Aidan wasn't arguing. He liked the way she was bad-mouthing him.

'But he said I knew this Deegan. How could I?'

Jade's face wrenched.

'Do we have to talk about this? Let's forget about Elmwood, just for today.'

When the ferry pulled away from the landing stage they made their way to the rail to squint against the river spray. Corny stuff, but it felt the right thing to do.

I'm glad we came,' she said.

Aidan let his hand steal along her spine. She didn't pull away. They stood that way and watched the grey water churning. He was almost holding his breath, willing the moment to last as long as it could. He'd held on to Jade, Soft Version, for a whole five minutes and he liked it. She talked about herself, the music she listened to, even the books she read. He did his best not to look surprised when she reeled off the titles.

'You didn't have me down as a reader, did you?' she said.

Aidan shrugged. Why shouldn't she like reading?

'They sell the classics for a pound each in this remainder shop in town. I get them on the quiet. My friends don't know. They'd skit me if they did. I read for hours in bed every night.'

'Your guilty secret?' Aidan said.

'Something like that.'

She turned and fixed him with those deep brown eyes.

'What's your favourite book?' she asked. 'Oh yes, *Lord of the Rings*. I got you on that the other night.'

He had a lot favourites but he didn't want to talk about himself.

'You?' he asked.

'*Jane Eyre*,' Jade said, 'And *Tess of the D'Urbervilles*. Yes, I like Tess best. Have you read either of them?'

Aidan shook his head. He was starting to feel stupid. Then the ferry jogged his memory.

'I've read Roger McGough,' he said. '*The Stowaways*.'

'Oh, when they run away to sea,' Jade said, 'but end up going back and forth across the Mersey instead. I wouldn't mind running away.'

'We could do it now,' Aidan said. 'Let's hijack this one and take off for the South Seas.'

Jade laughed.

'Where would we go?'

'Tahiti. You'd look great in a grass skirt.'

She shook her head.

'You've got a one track mind.'

He looked at Liverpool. There was a time these nine miles of dockland served merchant shipping from all over the world. Granddad had gone on about it often enough. He was defiantly proud of his Liverpool, but the city he'd known was gone forever. Now the waterfront was mostly empty. For years Liverpool had lost its reason to live. Some travel writer said the place had more past than future. Standing on the deck of the ferry, it seemed about right.

'What's it like,' Jade asked suddenly, 'Where you live?'

She turned to face him. His hand slid from her back, flopping uselessly and the spell was broken.

'Boring most of the time.'

'I bet you've got a big house.'

The North–South divide was never as big as most people thought, but in this case Jade wasn't far off. In his mind's eye Aidan pictured home: a four-bedroomed detached with its own pebbled driveway. It had double-glazing, a double garage, decking in the back garden. It was quiet, suburban, respectable, everything Elmwood Street wasn't. On Sundays the family would have lunch at Carsley Lock and watch people sculling on the river.

'It's all right, nothing special.'

He didn't feel comfortable on this terrain. Streetwise is cool. Suburban is . . . not.

'It's much like anywhere else,' he said. 'I bet Liverpool's got its leafy suburbs too.'

Jade shrugged. It was obvious she hadn't seen much of them.

'You know what?' she said. 'I've done more since I met you than I have with Mum in years. She just sits in front of the telly and gets rotten.'

'Rotten?'

'Drunk.'

'What about your dad?' Aidan asked.

'I don't have a dad,' she said, her eyes settling on him unflinchingly. 'Just a world-record collection of uncles. My real dad cleared off before I was born.'

She tossed her hair.

'Do you believe in love?' she asked suddenly.

This was a surprise. You never knew which Jade you were getting. Aidan had thought he knew the Jade he wanted; honest, beautiful and bright. All of a sudden, the Soft Version posed problems of its own. What Aidan wanted was fun. Nothing heavy. Certainly nothing to do with love. It was a very big word built out of four little letters.

'*Believe* in it?' he said. 'You make it sound like a religion.'

Unsure how to answer, he went for flip.

'Load of bull,' he said.

He wanted to change the subject. Jade didn't.

'Why is it?'

'Loving one person forever,' he said, putting a sneer in his voice.

He half-hoped she didn't believe him, but he couldn't bring myself to say how he really felt. She had her self-defence mechanisms, he had his.

'I mean, come on.'

Aidan thought of Mum and Dad. They were together but they didn't show their feelings all that much. It was hardly *Wuthering Heights*, more Blithering Middles. He looked at Jade and saw the disappointment in her face. He wanted to see the smile return to her eyes but there was no way back.

'Jeez,' he said, reeling in surprise. 'You believe in it, don't you, the whole thing?' In spite of himself he burst out laughing. He didn't like the sound of his voice. It was the big cheese at Greenwood School he was hearing, the act he put on to be life and soul of the party. But he couldn't stop. Jade bent under his scorn.

'Crazy, isn't it?' she said, her voice quavering slightly. 'I should know better, what with my mother. She's a sucker for love. She reads her Mills and Boons and she wants her tall, dark stranger, but her men always fall short. There's a new one nearly every week, slimeballs the lot of them. They just use her. Still, it would be great if it was true.'

There was a kind of desperation in her eyes. Aidan half-wished he'd answered differently. She wanted her mirage of love. What harm would it do to humour her? It might even earn him some valuable Brownie points. But it was too late to put it right. He was stuck for something to say. It didn't matter. Jade took the initiative. She reached up and laced her fingers behind his neck. Her eyes studied his face.

'You can kiss me if you want . . . even if you don't believe in love.'

He tried to say something back but his voice tightened up. Jade laughed, then her eyes went serious. She seemed to reach out for him with every atom of her being. Her hair, her exposed, tanned throat, her startling brown eyes transmitted hot, pulsating life. He felt her lips against his. She melted against him and he felt ten feet tall.

When they walked off the ferry they were holding hands. Excitement roared through his chest. She didn't seem disappointed any more. Maybe he'd felt this good before, but he really couldn't remember when. The feeling didn't last. They were walking across the Pier Head when his mobile rang. It was Emily. Jade read the name on the display screen and her face stiffened. Her hand slipped from his.

'Answer it,' she said.

'Hi Emily.'

He tried turning away from Jade but she could hear every word he said. His skin was crawling.

'Are you missing me, Ady?' Emily asked.

Aidan glanced at Jade. Oh, why this now?

'I suppose.'

The words fell apart in his mouth. There was a shocked silence at the other end.

'Aidan, are you all right?'

'Sure. Why wouldn't I be?'

There was another silence. Emily didn't know what to say. Oh, I can't stand this, he thought. He didn't want to hurt anybody's feelings.

'Yes, I'm fine.'

He tried to move away from Jade. His voice fell to a whisper.

'And yes, I miss you.'

Like hell he did! All memory of her face had vanished the first time he saw Jade. Emily was a name and a voice and that's all she was.

'Me too,' she oozed, relief eddying out of the handset.

When Aidan cut the call he tried to talk to Jade but she'd put a wall up.

'You know how it is,' he said.

'Do I?'

'I'm not going to break it off with her over the phone.'

'You're not going to break it off at all,' Jade retorted, a catch in her voice. 'Why should you?'

He knew the look in her eyes, the fractured dreams, the disappointment. Her mum was responsible for that and he wasn't good enough or understanding enough to make a difference.

'This was only ever going to be a bit of a laugh,' she said, the hard edge taking over. 'I'm your bit on the side. We both know that. You'll only be with me a few days. Then it's back to her.'

'But I don't want to be with her,' he protested. 'It's you I . . . like.'

The last word fell like a stricken bird. It certainly wasn't going to send her heart into a flutter. She needed so much more and he just couldn't provide it. Jade walked away, arms crossed, head bowed.

'Whatever.'

They got the bus home. All these bus journeys were a new experience for him. Most times back home Mum or Dad ferried him about and he lived walking distance from school. Buses belong to old Ealing comedies, ancient history. The scruffy single-decker they caught came as a bit of a shock. It was like a cattle truck. People filled the aisle: women with kids, men with boxes, old folks with rheumy eyes and shaky legs. It was hot and stuffy but that wasn't the worst of it. It was so packed it was impossible to talk. He reached for Jade's hand but she pulled it away. He got the message and gave up his seat for an old lady. She was grateful, so grateful he realised it didn't happen often.

He leaned over and hissed across at Jade:

'I'm sorry, OK?'

'What are you sorry for?' she asked.

There was a moment's silence then the accusation:

'You don't even know, do you?'

She stared stubbornly out of the window. The old lady met his eye and smiled sympathetically. He pulled a bit of a face and she laughed. Jade gave them both daggers looks. Then she leapt up and pushed past the old lady.

'Where are you going?' he asked.

'Away from you.'

She shoved her way down the bus.

'Jade!'

He followed her off the bus. They were a couple of stops from Elmwood.

'Jade,' he said, catching up with her. 'This is stupid. I couldn't just tell her I was finishing with her, not over the phone.'

Jade kept walking.

'Give me a break, will you?' he cried. 'I hate all this. I hate upsetting you. I hate going behind Emily's back. I . . .'

'Is that all you ever say?' Jade snapped. 'I, I, I. You're one selfish get, Aidan. You know why you don't love anybody? You're too in love with yourself to let anybody else in.'

OK, so it was a like a line from a cheesy soap opera, but it did for him. He sank into shocked silence. Nobody, but nobody, had ever sliced him open the way she had. It was a while before he set off after her.

'Jade . . .'

She didn't so much as turn her head.

'Drop dead,' she snapped.

'Jade.'

This time the language was stronger. She screamed her anger at him, same as she had screamed at her mother.

'You just want to use me, the way those men use Mum.'

Aidan froze on the spot.

'Use you? What do you mean?'

Jade tossed her black hair.

'What do you think I mean?'

He was about to follow her when he stopped in his tracks. He saw somebody he recognised, the driver of the blue BMW. He was standing across the road on a street corner. It looked as if he was killing time. Aidan glanced around for the car. He remembered the name Paul Gorman had told him: Deegan. Taking care not to attract the driver's attention he walked up the road a way and crossed. Falling in behind two men with dogs he made his way back. Aidan was now on the other side of the street from the driver. He turned left and froze. The BMW was parked between two other cars. The man in black was inside. So was Mum.

Seven

Coward.

It was Sunday morning and Aidan was staring into the bathroom mirror.

Coward.

There was emptiness in the eyes that looked back at him. He hardly knew the reflected face. Anxiety lived there, unease, maybe even fear. The truth was screaming at him; all his life he'd had it easy. Only child, doted on by loving parents, a well-off kid in a well-off corner of a well-off county, living the suburban lifestyle. He got everything he wanted: best trainers, latest gadgets, you name it, snap your fingers and it was there. He was one of the lucky few. No kidding, he might not always want to admit it, but his bit of Surrey was milk and honey on wheels. Were there times he felt ever so slightly smug? You betcha! All the kids at school were the same. What did they want to be after uni? Rich, that's what. But suddenly he didn't feel so lucky. He felt like crap.

He'd hardly slept and that was new, too. He'd seen one o'clock, two o'clock come up on his bedside clock. He'd tossed and turned, gone to the bathroom for cotton wool to stuff in his ears. But sounds you can block out; thoughts come seeping back. He'd seen the blue BMW float round the walls followed by other images: that man talking to Mum, his head close to hers, his dark eyes, his mouth making the shape of the words *You don't know me but I know you.* Aidan's mind had filled with shadows, one darker, more sharply focused than all the others. Nothing in his life so far had prepared him for the journey his thoughts were taking. Frightening new ideas had come one after the other, thudding like the blades of a knife-thrower around him. He twisted and turned as each one landed. Even then, as he stared into the mirror, his face seemed to melt into a smear of pain.

Then that other mind-clip had come, the one from his nightmares, of a younger Aidan running down a passage, bursting into a room to see a white figure crucified on a cross of flame. Even as the figure screamed out of the darkness, part ghost, part man, he was falling, falling, blood puddling around his head. The old, primal fear came. Was it Dad? No, not Dad, not his father. He was still standing, unharmed. In his half-waking state, Aidan clawed at the walls of his own mind, grasping after reality. Dad. But what about Dad? There he was, half a world away, making money for his family and this was what he got in return. Aidan's eyes shifted. He couldn't meet his own gaze.

Coward.

Aidan couldn't even stand up for Dad. He should have confronted her there and then while she sat in the car with *him*. That would have shown her! He could at least have said something when she got back, half an hour after he did. But he didn't open his mouth. All he did was fight the shake in his voice and go off to bed like Mum's good little boy, Mum's good, cowardly little boy. His own mother having an affair? It was sick. This happened in other families, not his, not his mother, his father. How long had it been going on? Those times she came to see Gran and Granddad on her own, was it then? Was that what the visits were really about? Or did it go back even longer? Was this slimeball, this 2D, cardboard cut-out man in black some kind of childhood sweetheart? It all seemed so far-fetched. Parents only did this on TV or in the tabloids. Hell, he was living a soap opera.

But he'd seen her.

He'd watched the scumbag reach out and curl a lock of hair over her ear. He didn't hang round after that. This was his mother. Some things you just don't want to see.

He ran.

He even ran past Jade. He heard her calling after him. He didn't stop though. He was the little boy in the nightmare. His feet hit the pavement the same way. His heart beat the same way. He ran and ran until he thought his heart was going to burst. Then he slumped to the ground in some filthy back alley and knuckled his eyes like a little kid. That's right, he sobbed himself dry, stuck on a skewer of rage and self-pity. He felt the burn of humiliation. He thought of kids in school whose parents had split up. Some it didn't seem to affect. Maybe they were putting on a performance, how was he supposed to know? It wasn't as though he had ever given it much thought. But they weren't the ones he was thinking about. It was the others, the ones who did let it show. He remembered the expression on their faces, as though they were disintegrating from the inside. Was that going to be him?

Sometimes, while he was tossing and turning, disgust and curiosity fighting inside him, he imagined what it might be like if they split up. He'd be expected to live with Mum. He'd resent her and make her life a misery, throw it back in her face every chance he got. Dad would get a flat. That's the way it worked, wasn't it, the man moved into a flat and saw the kids at the weekend? Mark Shaw was a good father, so maybe Aidan would see him a couple of times a week. A ghost walked through him. How could he be thinking like this? He had to do something about it. He had to confront Mum. But the very thought of it made him feel weightless, not part of anything. How do you do it? How do you go up to your own mother and accuse her of betrayal? He couldn't. He didn't have the words.

Coward.

He got downstairs and breathed a sigh of relief. Mum and Gran were out. He remembered something, a fragment of the conversations that had swum around him half the evening. They were going to decorate the living room. *Brighten the place up.* Yes, a tin of paint, that would make Granddad's cancer go away. Aidan was supposed to help. He looked round at the house. Gran's influence was everywhere. The place was meticulous: mugs were stationed on coasters; newspapers were filed in a wooden rack; family photos were neatly arranged; surfaces were dust free. It could have belonged in a time capsule; the modern age perfectly preserved. Organised. Comfortable. Happy. Just one thing – in the corner an old man was dying. The order she had stamped on the house couldn't do anything about that. The old man was a reminder: some things you just can't tidy away.

'Are you OK, Aidan?' Granddad asked.

Aidan nodded.

'I should be asking you that.'

'Don't bother,' Granddad said. 'That's all I ever hear these days. Sure, I feel like saying, hunky dory except for this bloody lump that's eating me from the inside out.' It was the first time Aidan had heard him really angry. He noticed the green corduroy trousers Granddad was wearing.

The raised wales of the material were rubbed flat. They were worn out, just like him.

'I was sitting out the front one day. Her from number nineteen, O'Connor, the nosy one, you know what she did?'

Aidan shook his head.

'She asked your gran how I was doing. That's right, she talked over my head as though I was sodding simple or something! You know what I did, lad, I told her I've lost the lining of my lungs, not my marbles.'

'What did she say?'

'Not much she could say. She went off in a huff.'

Granddad chuckled, then coughed violently.

'Seriously though, you look a bit down in the mouth. What's wrong?'

Aidan felt a tingle of unease.

'I bet it's Jade,' Granddad said. 'I'm right, aren't I?'

Aidan didn't contradict him. It was better than the truth.

'Stay away from her, lad. She's going the same way as that mother of hers. It isn't her fault, poor kid. She never stood a chance.'

'How do you mean?'

Granddad's eyes searched his.

'You've seen how they live, haven't you? Everybody round here talks about them. You've been inside the house?'

Aidan nodded. Granddad's eyes seemed to swivel in his direction, flashing a warning. 'That isn't a home. It's a doss house. That's what Maggie Thatcher and her shower gave us: communities destroyed, people living off benefit, drug dealing on the street corner. The likes of Jade's mother, they've lost all self-respect, all hope. They just bump along, going from one man to another, all of them losers.'

Aidan felt himself drifting away. The words rolled by him, a rumble of well-worn complaints. Politics wasn't his thing at all. He was with Dad. If you worked hard, you'd be OK. Britain was full of opportunities if you knew where to look. Everybody gets what they deserve. 'No such thing as society?' Granddad said. 'There isn't any more, thanks to her.'

He meant Mrs Thatcher, not Jade or her mum. Dad wouldn't have liked hearing this. He thought Mrs T was the beginning of Britain's climb back to prosperity, though he'd voted for New Labour at the last election. You wouldn't catch Granddad doing either. Aidan had heard all his lectures before, the way he had heard his tales of Bill Shankly, Liverpool and the Kop, every time Granddad came to visit. Granddad should have had his own soap box, Dad always said when he'd gone. He'd been a raving lefty at one time, the old guy. But what good did it do? It was ancient history, that's all. It belonged to the days of black and white TV. Then Aidan realised a living piece of that ancient history was talking to him.

'You're not listening, are you?'

Aidan came back from his daydream.

'What? Oh, sorry.'

Granddad's eyes burned as though all the sadness of the city had been rubbed in them. He'd got used to being ignored.

'Don't be,' he said. 'Just stay away from young Jade Harding, if you know what's good for you. She'll go the same way as that mother of hers.'

Aidan didn't know what was good for him, of course. Half an hour later, Mum still wasn't back. He wandered out into the street. He looked across at Jade's house. The curtains were drawn. Sunday morning. Nobody was up.

'You won't see her,' somebody said. 'Not this side of midday.'

It was Paul Gorman.

'How do you know?' Aidan snapped.

'Touchy, aren't you? I know what they're like, that's all.' Aidan went eye-to-eye with Paul. Straight away he wished he hadn't. Talk about fish eyes! There was no give, no hint of a flinch.

'You got a problem?' Paul said, his voice hardening.

'No, I just don't like the way you talk about Jade.'

Paul gave a low whistle.

'Don't tell me you've got the hots for her,' he said.

He made a show of examining Aidan's face.

'Yes, you look like you've got it bad.'

Aidan heard that low, humourless laugh of his.

'Still, if you're looking for a bit of fun you could do worse.'

Aidan felt uncomfortable being around Paul. Every time he met him the same suspicion bled into his mind. He gave a tight smile. Better than fighting. Paul started to walk away.

Aidan hated himself.

Coward.

But not a complete one.

'Who's Deegan?' he asked.

Paul spun round.

'This some kind of joke?'

'No,' Aidan said. 'No joke.'

Paul's eyes fastened on Aidan's. They were serious for a moment, then they relaxed.

'You're serious, aren't you? You don't know.'

He laughed out loud.

'So tell me,' Aidan insisted. 'Who is Deegan?'

Paul was about to speak. Then the look swam away.

He'd thought better of it. 'Ask your old lady,' Paul said.

Aidan felt a sheen of sweat on his face and back. He balled his fist and yelled after Paul as he turned the corner.

'Tell me!'

Paul looked back and shook his head. Then he was gone.

That day Aidan was directionless. He didn't go swimming. He didn't use his Saveaway to see the sights. He didn't go looking for Jade. In the end she came looking for him. She found him sitting on a wall at the top of the street.

'Do you want some company?' she asked.

Aidan shaded his eyes to look at her. The sun was behind her, leaving her silhouetted against the light. He didn't answer. He just shuffled along to make space for her.

'Is this about yesterday?' she said.

'I don't get you.'

'This, the silent treatment.'

'Oh. No.'

'I'm sorry anyway,' she said. 'I've got a foul temper, just like my mum.'

'I asked for it.'

She wasn't arguing.

'Still,' she said. 'I'm the one who said it was a bit of fun in the first place. I can hardly blame you for taking me at my word.'

She waited a beat, probably so he could contradict her, tell her she was the only one. Beneath the tough veneer, she was brittle as glass. Aidan remembered what Granddad said. She would go the same way as her mother. He didn't say anything to reassure her. He wasn't in the mood. Jade picked up the thread of what she was saying. 'I don't know what I was getting so angry about.'

He looked straight ahead. Any other time he would have

been trying to make it up to her. For once he wasn't thinking about Jade. His mind was crowded with images of the blue BMW, Mum, the man in black – mostly of the pair of them together.

'Has something happened?' Jade asked. 'You're not listening to me.'

Aidan gave a low chuckle.

'You want to know what's the matter?' he said. 'I just got my guts kicked out.'

She gave him a look that said: *welcome to my world.* That humbled him. Much as he'd tried to avoid it, he'd always felt kind of superior until that moment. He had it all, didn't he: the big house, the two new cars in the driveway, two parents (still married). He had the whole package.

'Do you want to tell me about it?'

'Not really.'

'Suit yourself,' Jade said.

She wasn't being huffy, just matter-of-fact. He could suit himself. He did. It's the weirdest thing, he couldn't talk to Mum, but he could talk to Jade. He'd never found anyone this easy to talk to, not even Chris or Emily, not even Dad.

'It's my mum,' he said. 'I saw her with somebody.'

'Who?'

'The man I asked you about, Deegan.'

She stared back at him, forehead rumpling.

'And?'

Did he have to spell it out?

'And he isn't my dad.'

'You mean, you think she's messing about?'

His heart jolted.

'What else can it be? She was in his car. They had somebody looking out.'

Jade's eyes clouded with caution.

'You what? They had a look out?'

'That's right.'

Her face was unreadable.

'What's wrong?' Aidan said.

'Nothing. Just doesn't sound like they're having an affair, does it? It's not the sort of thing you drag a third person in to, is it?'

He gave a *beats me* shrug.

'I don't know,' he said. 'I don't have anything to go on.'

'Well you don't. An affair is secret. That's the whole point.'

'If you say so.'

'Listen,' Jade said. 'I asked Mum. She thinks she remembers Deegan.'

'And?'

'I don't think it's good. Mum had a boyfriend round, so it was hard to get much sense. I didn't get any further than the stuff I've already told you. I'll find out for you though.'

Aidan felt a surge of gratitude. That's when he looked at Jade properly for the first time. She was wearing a cream and green dress and white trainers, all Ellesse.

'Looking good,' he said.

'Thanks,' she said, moving closer. 'Want to do something?'

By way of answer he took her hand.

'Let's go.' They got back about six in the evening. It wasn't as though they'd done anything special but they had been together, and that's what mattered. The first thing he saw when they turned into Elmwood was the newspaper taped all over the bay window of number 66.

'Oh great!'

'What's the matter?'

'I was supposed to help decorate.'

'So go and decorate.'

Aidan looked at Jade and smiled.

'You're great, you know that?'

She flicked back her hair. Aidan realised they'd been together hours and she hadn't once put on the streetwise act.

'Will I see you later?' he asked.

'Will you be finished in time?' she countered.

'If that's what I have to do to see you then yes, I'll be finished.'

Judging by the look on Mum's face she was in the mood for a fight. Gran caught her eye and stopped her in her tracks.

'I was out with Jade,' Aidan said. 'We lost track of time. Sorry.'

'Can you paint the ceiling?' Gran asked, still darting warning glances in Mum's direction. 'Us little people can't reach.'

Mum took the hint. She was probably going to catch him on his own later. Not one to let things drop, his mum.

'Sure,' Aidan said. 'No problem. Have you got any overalls?'

'You can use your Granddad's,' Gran said.

She told him where to find them. He managed to wriggle into them but the trousers ended half way down his calves. Everybody laughed, even Mum, and she was doing her serious, disapproving bit.

'You look like Charlie Chaplin,' was Gran's verdict.

'Weren't his trousers too long?' Aidan said.

Gran shrugged.

'You know what I mean.'

Aidan didn't mind painting. It was relaxing in a mindless way. He plugged himself into his MP3 player and got on

72

with it. Good as Snow Patrol were, the music wasn't completely successful. The image of Mum and the man in black still swam round in his mind. He wanted to ask Mum about it, but how? How on earth do you ask about something like that? Still, the shock of seeing her with him didn't burst into his mind with quite the same force. He was learning to live with it, whatever it was.

He was painting the coving when Gran came in with a can of Lilt and a sandwich. Aidan took a bite.

'You got chorizo!'

'You said you liked it.'

'But Gran, you didn't need to go straight out and get it. Where did you find it?'

'We do have Tesco up here,' she said. 'It's not quite the outer limits.'

'No,' he said. 'Anyway, I'm nearly done. What time is it?'

'Nine,' said Gran. 'Why? Do you want to see that girl again?'

Aidan took a swig of the Lilt.

'That's the idea.'

'Just watch yourself, lad,' Gran said. 'I don't want you getting your feelings hurt.'

'Why has everybody got such a downer on Jade?' he asked.

'Not my place to say,' she replied.

'Go on, spit it out, Gran.'

She took his empty plate.

'She's not too choosy about the company she keeps – that Gorman lad for starters.'

He felt that prickle of anxiety again.

'Go on.'

But Gran's voice crumpled like a paper bag.

'If you can't see it, I can't tell you.'

73

'Is that it?' he asked. 'Are you finished?'

'Jade's trouble,' Gran said, finally, taking the plate back to the kitchen. 'Don't say you haven't been warned.'

Warned is one thing. Believing it is another. Aidan showered and put on jeans and a white tee-shirt. He thought Jade would approve. He was still looking for her when he spotted the blue BMW. It rolled into the street in second gear. He stepped back into an alleyway and watched. The car came about halfway down the street, then stopped. Paul Gorman crossed the road and poked his head through the open window.

Something was exchanged.

'Is that him?' a voice asked.

Aidan looked round.

'Jade.'

His voice was shaky. He didn't like people creeping up on him.

'You didn't half give me a fright.'

Jade didn't answer. She was looking at the car. 'That's the man you're talking about?'

'Yes.'

Aidan heard the air escaping from her lips.

'You know him?'

'I asked around.'

'And?'

'It's like I told you. He's not a nice man.'

'Jade,' he said, the ghost of a laugh in his voice. 'I've figured that out for myself.'

'OK,' Jade said. 'You want the gory details? He's a villain. Drugs, knock-off, armed robbery, he's done it all. He hasn't been round for a while. Kicking his heels abroad, that's what the rumours say. That must be why I didn't recognise the name. Mum did. She went to the same school as him. He's a couple of years younger. Mum wasn't big on details but there's something else. Something happened years ago. There's bad blood with the Geraghtys.'

'Who are they?'

'Dealers. Real pond life. Word is, they're into shooters big style. If you lived round here you'd have heard of the Geraghtys all right.'

Aidan absorbed the names but nothing made sense. Jade finished her story.

'It seems Deegan's come back to reclaim his turf from the Geraghtys.'

A shiver cut through him. He asked the obvious question.

'What's Mum doing with a man like that?'

Only he didn't really want an answer.

Eight

Aidan shuddered away the white figure, the flame. The thud of the figure hitting the ground was still with him when he woke. So were the echoes of his screams. It wasn't like the old movies where the hero wakes up screaming. Aidan wasn't wide-eyed with terror. There was no scream to bring Mum running. All there was was a deep, cold, numbing depression. The dream meant something. It was a splinter lodged right in his very core. Since coming to Liverpool, he was having the nightmare more often. He was beginning to dread going to sleep. In the bathroom he washed the sheen of sweat from his face. But nothing could sluice the shadows of that dream room from his mind. It weighed like a migraine. At breakfast next morning Mum had news.

'You'll be happy,' she said. 'We're going home tomorrow.'

'Tomorrow!'

The word came out in a gasp.

'We can't be.'

'Why not?'

For a few moments he didn't know what to say.

'I thought we were here for the fortnight.'

Inquisitive eyes settled on his face. She'd heard the protest in his voice.

'You've changed your tune,' she said. 'A few days ago I couldn't get you to come with me. All of a sudden you don't want to leave. What gives?'

Aidan was reacting the way you do when you're holding something back. Wilting under her look, he struggled to find an answer.

'It's a bit of a surprise, that's all.' He was still trying to come up with something, any reason that might make her change her mind, when the kettle boiled. She got up and made a coffee. He spoke to her back.

'Don't Gran and Granddad still need us here?'

Mum turned, leaning against the work surface, and sipped her coffee. Like Aidan she was dancing round the issues that mattered.

'We've done the decorating,' she said. 'I think it's time we got back for your dad. He should be home tomorrow. I'll be up again in a few weeks.'

Yes, Aidan thought, when I'm not with you. What's the matter, am I cramping your style? He remembered the other times she'd come up, always over the weekend, always alone.

'Has something happened?' he said.

Her eyes lost their focus and closed for an instant before she answered.

'Like what?'

Aidan let the question hang.

'Dunno,' he said, still the coward, still unable to ask her about *him*. 'Anything.'

'Your dad's coming home,' she replied, as though that was any kind of answer.

'You always knew when he was getting back,' Aidan said, stubborn without daring to be honest. 'So why are we cutting our visit short now?'

She started picking at her sleeve. Unease radiated from her.

'Come on, Mum,' he said. 'Talk to me. What's the hurry?'

'We're going,' she said. 'And that's that.'

She curled a lock of hair behind her ear. It reminded Aidan of that moment in the car with the man in black.

'Leave your clothes out on the bed,' she said. 'I'll pack this afternoon.' Aidan stood up, knocking his chair over. In his hurry to leave the room he almost collided with Gran.

'You're unbelievable,' he said, finally snarling his pathetic, helpless, truthless anger at Mum.

She was unbelievable all right . . . and he was a coward.

All that time in the kitchen he'd wanted to loose a stream of questions at her, about the man in black, and what she was doing with him. Equally, he'd wanted to shut out any replies she might offer. He was like a boxer trying to fight with one arm tied behind his back. He couldn't tell her what he knew. Anxiety lodged deep inside him like a seed. No matter what she did now, the seed could only grow. He stood out on the street and felt the sun on his skin. But it didn't warm him. The deep cold that had entered the marrow of his bones when he saw her with her cheap man in black was still with him.

With nothing to do, he went over to Jade's house. All the curtains were drawn. Sunday, Monday, it was all the same to them. Aidan dug his hands in his pockets and carried on walking. He thought about Mum and the man in black. Ever since he'd seen them together he'd thought about little else. He was scared that they had something going on. He was even more frightened by the alternative that Jade had hinted at: that an affair might be too easy an explanation. But what else could it be? He was turning the corner when he saw Gran hurrying his way.

'Something wrong?' he asked.

'No,' she said. 'I wanted a word, that's all.'

'Go on.'

'I don't know what you think is going on, Aidan,' she said. 'But you're wrong.' OK, he thought, so I'm wrong. What gives?

'Your mum's done what she can for now, that's all,' Gran said. 'It won't make any difference, keeping the pair of you here.'

The words just came tumbling out.

'She hasn't got anything to hide, if that's what you think. That's not why she's going.'

Aidan saw the way she searched his face. She seemed to want something from him.

He had nothing to offer.

'We'll see you again,' she said. 'Soon.'

She touched his arm.

'Jill loves the bones of you, you know.'

'Yes, I know.'

And he did. Nothing could change that. But it wasn't enough. You can love, betray, and still be loved.

'So you'll come back inside and have some breakfast?'

Aidan followed.

'You're OK now?' she said as they reached the front door. 'I've put your mind at rest?'

He gave a half nod. It's what she wanted and he was happy to play along. But the moment her back was turned he found himself frowning. The old girl had been trying way too hard.

Once back inside Aidan got the job of taking Granddad his cup of tea. Granddad didn't eat that much. At least, Aidan never saw him eat. He seemed to live on air. Granddad said thanks with a voice like a file on metal. It was high and sharp as if the top varnish of life had flaked off it. Aidan had only been around the house a few days but he knew that voice, so different to the usual low burr. It meant he'd had a bad night. He hadn't slept much and he was in pain.

'Getting to you, isn't it?' Aidan said.

Talk about a master of understatement.

'It's not right, you know,' Granddad said, shifting in his chair. 'Forty five years I worked, man and boy, and look at me now. Just when I should be enjoying life I'm as weak as a baby. I'm sodding useless like this.'

He took a shallow breath.

'This . . . it isn't living. I'm coming apart at the ruddy seams because of the filth I had to work in. I paid my stamp, raised a family, never lifted a hand to your grand-mother.'

He let his head loll back. He was trying not to let the discomfort show.

'And this is how I end up.'

He turned his head and his sunken eyes swept the street.

'Out there,' he said. 'Any time of the day you can see the scum of the Earth, poisoning the city with drugs and crime and, you know what, they're loving it. They've no shame. They've got the morals of sewer rats. When I was young I thought we were working for a decent future. Can you credit it, Aidan? I thought I'd live to see a better world. Now look at it.'

He seemed to realise he was sinking into self-pity. He managed a last observation.

'No justice, is there?'

'No,' Aidan said, mired in his own boggy patch of misery, 'I don't suppose there is.'

He turned to go but Granddad had a parting shot.

'Don't give your mother grief,' he said. 'She does her best for you.'

First Gran, now you. Aidan glanced back and smiled,

but the moment he was out of the room the smile slid from his face.

The phone rang at about half past eleven. Aidan was expecting Dad. He'd be calling to say he was on his way home.

'Yes?'

'Could I speak to Jill?'

It was a woman's voice.

'Sure. Who's speaking?'

'Tell her it's Carol Flaherty.'

He did a double-take. Here he was talking to a figment of the imagination. For days he'd had this Carol Flaherty down as some kind of stupid alibi, now he was talking to her.

'Right,' he said, getting over the surprise. 'I'll get her for you.'

He found Mum sitting with Granddad. She had his bony hands between hers. They exchanged glances and she went to the phone.

'Who is this Carol woman?' he asked.

Granddad didn't look at him.

'She was at the same school as your mum,' he said.

Aidan noticed that he didn't say: *went to school with your mum*. They weren't close then.

'Are they friends?'

The answer stalled.

'Yes . . . something like that.'

Aidan wasn't going to get anything else out of Granddad, same way he didn't get anything from anyone. It was at that moment something snapped. Even cowards have their breaking point, and this was his. He'd hit the wall of silence once too often. By the time he caught up with Mum she had put the phone down. She had her car keys in her hand.

'Where are you going?' he asked.

'To see Carol. I won't be long.'

She was at the door before he said it:

'Does this have something to do with a man in a blue BMW?'

She stiffened. There, he'd finally plucked up the courage to say it. There was no going back.

'What?'

'You heard.'

When she turned to look at him he could see the conflicting emotions in her face.

'How . . . ?'

He felt like laughing. What was she going to come out with next: who, where and why?

'I saw you with him.'

'What are you talking about?'

'On Saturday, down that side street, the one opposite the church.'

His eyes locked hers.

'You were having a really cosy chat.'

She brushed back her hair.

'It's not what you think.'

That just made it worse, the way she slipped into the stupid, knee-jerk response.

'No? So what is it?'

'I didn't want you to find out like this,' she murmured, as if sleep-walking. 'Look, I'll talk to you when I get back.'

'Why not now?' he said.

'Aidan,' she said, surprisingly softly given the way he was pursuing her. 'Just be a little bit patient.'

She put her hand to his face.

'I'll be half an hour, an hour at most. Please.'

His silence was all the answer she needed. He watched her go.

He didn't wait in for her. He couldn't. Hanging round for Mum, knowing his grandparents were watching him, most likely knowing what she had to tell him but not letting on, it would all have been too much. He decided to call for Jade. Her mother came to the door. He could smell the cigarette smoke on her breath and her clothes.

'Is Jade home?'

'She went out.'

She was big on nicotine, short on conversation.

'Do you know where she went?'

A shake of the head.

'She doesn't tell me.'

'Oh, well thanks anyway.'

For nothing.

Aidan had gone a couple of steps when she said something that stopped him in his tracks.

'I think I heard someone earlier. It might have been Paul.'

'Paul Gorman?'

'That's him.' It didn't take long to find them. They were by the Overhead Railway. He spotted them from fifty yards away. They seemed to be having a quarrel.

'What are you doing with him?' Aidan yelled, causing them to turn.

The blood drained from Jade's face.

'It's not what you think.'

'Everybody seems to be saying that today,' he sneered.

He saw the confusion in her face.

'What?'

He didn't explain. He was more interested in what she was doing with Paul, who as usual seemed to find the situation funny.

'What are you laughing at?' Aidan said.

Paul took note of the resentment and replied with a superior:

'That's for you to find out.'

Aidan swore at him, told him to go. Paul's fixed, goading smile didn't waver.

'Just clear off, will you?' Aidan repeated.

Paul was enjoying it.

'Make me,' he said.

'Oh, stop it,' Jade said. 'You're pathetic, both of you.'

'No,' Aidan said. 'What's pathetic is you hanging round with scum like him.'

'You watch your mouth,' said Paul, showing the first signs of irritation.

Which is when Aidan made his big mistake. He forgot he wasn't talking to his usual crowd back home. There he was top dog. Here, well, his bark didn't scare Paul. He was a mad dog himself.

'What's the weather like on Planet Moron?' Aidan said. 'What's wrong, don't you understand simple English?' He put on his best Neanderthal voice and faked dragging his knuckles on the ground. Aidan could be really subtle sometimes.

'Well,' he said, 'What are you hanging round for? I thought I told you to clear off.'

The veins in Paul's temple bulged like fat, blue worms. Then pain erupted around Aidan. Paul slammed his fist into Aidan's face. Blood roared in his ears as he tried to shake away the numbness in his head. His arms were flailing against Paul's taut, hard figure as he tried to pull him in close, stop the punches. Paul hit Aidan again and pain ripped through him a second time. His face went numb. A split-second later, he felt his legs buckle. Then Paul had him up against the security boards that were nailed to the Overhead Railway's ground floor windows.

'Before you go mouthing off again,' Paul snarled, shaking Aidan like a rag doll, 'you should find out who you're talking to.'

Aidan tried to twist away but Paul's hand was like a vice. Aidan saw Jade tugging at Paul's arm. She was trying to haul Paul off him.

'I don't care who your father is,' Paul spat, shoving his face into Aidan's. 'You don't ever talk that way to me again. Got it?'

Weak with fear and burning with humiliation, Aidan nodded. Paul let him go. He was done and started to walk away.

'Wait,' Aidan said, panting between the words. 'What you just said, about not caring who my father is.'

'Yes?'

The earth was yawning open at his feet.

'What did you mean?'

'Work it out.' Aidan was falling forward into emptiness. He dreaded the knowledge that was waiting for him but he had to face it.

'Tell me!'

'You can't be that stupid, can you?'

He was laughing at Aidan, revelling in the look of misery on his face.

'It's Deegan, creep. He's your dad. That's right, your old lady's been around the block a few times. Right old bike when she was younger, so they say. Didn't know that, did you?'

Aidan reached out to steady himself against the wall. The world seemed to sway around him.

'You're lying!'

'Why should I? It's no secret. It's the talk of the street. First Sean Deegan comes home, then his woman and son follow. Bit of a coincidence, don't you think? Maybe he wants to play Happy Families.'

Aidan stared at Jade.

'Did you know about this?'

She nodded.

'I heard. Oh, Aidan, I'm sorry. I didn't know how to tell you.'

He didn't say another word. He just ran. The street was whirling out of control. He reached the house and hammered on the door. Somebody snapped the locks from the inside. The door opened and there was Mum.

'Is it true?'

Her eyes widened at his appearance.

'Have you been fighting?'

'This Deegan, is it true?' He could see the emotions working in her face.

'Just tell me, is he my dad?'

'Who told you that?'

He wanted to swear at her, flay her with his words.

'What the hell does that matter? What difference does it make who told me? Is it true?'

'Not here,' she said, shoving him out into the street.

He started to resist, twisting away from her.

'Tell me!'

She unlocked the car with the key fob.

'Not here,' she said again. 'Think about your Granddad. If you care anything for your grandparents you'll shut up right now and come with me.'

She opened the door.

'Get in, Aidan. Please.'

He did as he was told and she drove.

'I just want to know what's going on,' Aidan said, finally getting a handle on his temper. 'Paul says this Sean Deegan's my dad. He can't be. He just . . .'

He was gulping down mouthfuls of air, as though it was in short supply.

'Tell me it isn't true.'

Mum tried to interrupt, to ask something about Paul Gorman. He ignored her.

'It's a filthy lie, isn't it? He's just a piece of crap trying to take a rise out of me. Tell me it isn't true.'

He was gabbling, incoherent. Most of all, he was desperate for it to be a lie. Even though, in his heart of hearts, he already knew the truth, he looked to Mum for reassurance. There was none. Without meeting his eyes she said simply: 'It's true.'

He sagged back into the passenger seat. For the next few minutes he watched north Liverpool flash by without a sound.

Mum stopped the car at Crosby Marina. Wind turbines turned over the Freeport. Seagulls fought and yelped overhead.

'Promise to let me talk,' she said, 'And I'll tell you everything.'

Aidan gave a scornful laugh.

'This should be interesting,' he said. 'You tell me nothing for fifteen years and now you're going to tell me *everything*. Well, aren't I the lucky one?'

'Aidan, calm down.'

That was the last thing he wanted to do.

'Why should I?'

'No interruptions,' she said. 'Promise.'

He turned away.

'Just say what you've got to.'

He could feel her eyes on him. Finally she started to speak.

'What you've been told is true,' she said. 'Sean Deegan's

your natural father, for what it's worth. He was my first boyfriend. I got pregnant. I'm not proud of it, but it happens to lots of girls. There isn't a teenager born yet who gets an A* in sex education. All of us fail somehow.'

He turned to look at her.

'And that's it?'

'I thought you weren't going to interrupt.'

She watched him for a few moments then softened. 'Aidan, this is really hard for me. Just give me some leeway. Please.'

He nodded.

'I was young,' she said. 'Not much older than you are now. I thought I was in love.'

She saw his expression change. Anger became revulsion.

'OK, I was stupid. Dad warned me off him but I wouldn't listen. Sean's trouble, but I just couldn't see it.'

'Well, I can,' Aidan said. 'Jade says he's a villain.'

'He was wild when I met him,' Mum said.

Wild! Well, that's one way of describing a drug-dealing psycho.

'But no more than that. I lived with him for eighteen months . . .'

'You what?'

'Yes, after you were born. We set up a flat in Kirkdale.'

Aidan was reeling. She had a whole life he knew nothing about. *He* had a life he knew nothing about. It was a while before he started making sense of what she was saying. 'Then I started hearing things. Bit by bit, I found out how he was making his money. I tried not to believe it – I was in love with him – but there was no other explanation. I found out he was dealing drugs. I even tried to tell myself it was just a bit of pot but he didn't even draw the line at the hard stuff. I know for a fact that he brought in at least one consignment of heroin. Gear, he called it. In the end, I just couldn't take it any more. Mum arranged for me to go and live with your Aunty Pat.'

'In America?'

'No, this was before they moved out there. At that time they lived in Surrey. Pat and her husband did so much. They put us up for a few months until I could get myself somewhere to live. Pat gave me some money. So did Mum and Dad.'

Guilt stained her features. 'It was money they didn't have. Anyway, with everybody's help I could put a roof over our heads, get childcare, go to college. I did my teacher training. It was a new start.'

Aidan stared in disbelief. This was like . . . what do they call it? False memory. There he was thinking he was Surrey born and bred, brought up in your classic nuclear family, and all the while there was this other past, the bit before the beginning. His back story.

'Away from Sean, I was able to put my life back together.'

'So where does Dad fit in to all this?'

'I went into college one Easter holiday to use the library. Mark was there attending a conference. It was just a casual meeting. It went from there.'

'He didn't mind you having a kid?'

'He was great about it. He seemed to revel in having a ready-made family. Mark has always been true as steel. He doted on you. All that stuff about blood being thicker than water, it's nonsense. Anybody can father a child. Raising one, that's another matter. Mark's always been there. He's the man who raised you, sat by your bed when you were ill. Even Dad likes him, despite the politics. He knows a good man when he sees one. Mark's your father, Aidan, not Sean.'

'You don't need to go on,' Aidan told her. 'I'm not stupid.'

He took a breath.

'Look, I don't need a lecture Mum. I think I can work out the rights and wrongs for myself. It's facts I want. You owe me that much.'

It was his turn to talk. He asked lots of questions and cut her short when she tried to dress it up. He wasn't interested in excuses. All the whys and wherefores could come later. After fifteen years in the dark, he deserved the truth. He wanted it simple, unadorned. When did they leave Liverpool? When did Dad – Mark Shaw – come into their lives? The funny thing, Mum seemed to go hazy on details here and there. Maybe she had a reason for acting vague. Either way, there was still something missing from her tale. He just didn't know what.

'What about this Carol Flaherty? Who's she?'

'Sean's sister.'

'Yes? So what did you want her for?'

'What do you think?' Mum said. 'I knew he'd approached you in the street. Granddad saw the car. I had to get him to stay away from us. Carol would know how to get in touch with him.'

'Is that why we're going?' he asked. 'Because he's come sniffing round?'

Mum went to reply but he cut her short.

'Or is there another reason?'

Horror rose in her face.

'What do you mean by that?'

'I saw him touch you.'

'Then you didn't stay to see what happened next,' Mum said. 'I slapped him.'

Aidan waited a beat.

'It's true,' she insisted, her eyes wide and pleading. 'I slapped him and got out of the car.'

Aidan felt hope flare inside him. Even now, after everything, he wanted to trust her.

'So you don't have any feelings for him?'

A pause, then:

'None at all. I love Mark.' And I love you, Aidan thought. In spite of the secrets, I do love you. How could it be otherwise?

'I need a hug,' Mum said.

Aidan smiled and held her.

'Do we still have to go home?' he asked, pulling away. 'Now that I know?'

Mum nodded.

'Yes,' she said. 'We're going home.'

Her answer troubled him. He had unfinished business with Jade.

The Gunslinger

He will get the call any time now. He knows what he has to do. He runs his finger along the row of books, his collection of nightmares and dreamscapes. You really know how to write, Mr King, he muses. He stops at *Misery*, slides the book from the shelf, and smiles to himself. He sees the man with his broken legs, the obsessive rescuer with her blowtorch. He can almost breathe the fear of the fallen man, the sense of power running through the veins of his guardian angel. That's the way of the world: predator and prey, hunter and hunted. But now the tables are turning. The hunter is about to be hunted. It has begun.

Nine

Unfinished business, that was the name of the game. Aidan lay in bed staring at the ceiling, unable to sleep or keep the suspicions out of his head. Voices floated up from the street. From time to time he got up and looked out. Figures slid by, picked out by the electric lights. The weather broke that Monday night. Rain peppered the darkened streets. He couldn't believe it. He was going back to his summer with Emily and Chris and he was sick at the thought of it. The world that had opened wide before him was shrinking to a puddle of suburban cosiness. They were leaving the next morning. By way of proof, his bag sat packed in the corner of the room.

'We can't go,' he murmured into the night. 'Not yet.'

It was half past twelve, maybe a quarter to one. It was quiet downstairs. He was about to go back to bed and have another try at getting off to sleep when he heard a car engine. The blue BMW pulled into the street. It prowled halfway down then stopped opposite the house.

'What's your game?' Aidan said out loud.

He watched. There were two men in the car: the driver and Sean Deegan. Aidan couldn't bring himself to call the man in black Dad. That would make him a freak of nature, a mistake. His head throbbed with the thud of his own blood. The street was calling. In that moment he made a decision. Pulling on his trackie bottoms and snatching a tee-shirt he padded downstairs.

'Trainers.'

He looked around the hallway floor. Where did he kick them off? Eventually he found them in the living room. That's when he became aware of a dark figure in the corner.

'Granddad!'

The old man's eyes were pools of shadow. 'You gave me a fright.'

'What are you doing up, Aidan?'

'I came down for something to drink.'

The old favourite. Granddad wasn't going to believe him but he said it anyway.

'Are you OK?' Aidan asked.

Granddad didn't answer.

'Go back to bed, Aidan. You don't want to see him.'

Aidan didn't deny it. Granddad knew Deegan was outside. He knew Aidan wanted to talk. Granddad knew it all.

'Go to your room, lad. Let things lie.'

Aidan nodded and stepped into the hallway. He had his trainers in his hand. Glancing in the direction of the living room he hesitated at the bottom of the stairs. He took a few heavy steps for Granddad's benefit then gripped the banister and swung himself lightly back down into the hall. Still listening for Granddad, Aidan pulled on his shirt and trainers. The front door would be a giveaway. Granddad would be bound to hear. Aidan padded into the kitchen and turned the key, wincing at the grating sound of the lock, then stepped out into the yard. Rain was drilling against the walls and windows. It was gushing in great, silvery gouts from the broken guttering and landing with a great splat on the concrete path. The feel of the cold, fat drops made him shiver but the rain was his friend. It would muffle the sounds of his footsteps. Easing open the gate he slipped into the alley.

Skin still prickling over the surprise Granddad had given him, Aidan walked down the alleyway and onto Elmwood, far enough up to be out of his sight if he was continuing his vigil at the front window. Aidan waited. It didn't take long for Deegan to see him. The car coasted down to Aidan and Deegan lowered the window. 'Get in.'

Aidan shook his head.

'You'll get soaked,' Deegan said.

'What's this?' Aidan answered. 'Sudden concern for my welfare?'

He did the spoiled American teenager bit.

'Aw shucks, after all this time I didn't know you cared.'

Deegan didn't show a flicker of emotion. There were no protests, no attempt at a defence.

'OK,' he said. 'Have it your way. I'll get out.'

He glanced at the driver. Aidan registered dark, slightly spiked hair and flat, unreadable features.

'I won't be long, Tone.'

A Scouse abbreviation, short for Tony, and unbelievably irritating.

'I'll be down the alley,' said Tony. 'I need a Jimmy.'

Jimmy Riddle. More slang. He needed to pee. He was about to go when Deegan caught his sleeve.

'No need to take the keys,' he said. 'I might want some music. Besides, we're getting soaked out here. I'm hoping my laddo here will get in the car.'

Tony hesitated then nodded.

'I'll leave them in the ignition.'

Tony stowed something in the glove compartment and walked towards the alley.

'Sure you don't want to sit in the car?' Deegan said.

'Tony's house-trained. He'll just hang around. He knows when to make himself scarce.'

Aidan put Tony to the back of his mind and fixed Deegan with a stare. His fleshy face was already shiny with the rain. 'So you're my natural father?'

He used Mum's words. They were neutral and that was good. The way Aidan was feeling, he would have preferred sperm donor. It suited him better. Deegan met his look. For a moment menace seemed to seep from his pores. Could be it was just his reputation? Fact is, Aidan was wary of him. Sullen fires lit in the pinpoint, obsidian eyes. No, Aidan was more than wary. My God, this thug was his father!

'Yes,' Deegan said. 'I'm your dad. Is there anything else you want to know?'

'I want to know what you're doing hanging round all the time.'

A smile hovered at the corner of his mouth.

'I heard Jill was back. I wanted to see you.'

'Why?'

'You're my son.'

Aidan rolled his eyes.

'That might sound more convincing if it hadn't taken you quite so long to say it.'

Deegan did something with his face too, the first sign of emotion. It said: fair point.

'So why are *you* here, Aidan?'

That was a good question, one which left Aidan struggling for an answer.

'I wanted to see you,' he admitted after a while. 'Curiosity maybe, though now I have I can't think why.'

There didn't seem anything else to say.

'We're leaving tomorrow,' he said.

Deegan was surprised.

'That right?'

Aidan nodded.

'Jill should have told me,' Deegan said.

'Why?' Aidan said. 'What does she owe you? You don't think you're going to get to know me, do you?'

Deegan didn't answer. Something had attracted his attention. He swung his gaze up the street.

'Did you hear that?'

'No,' Aidan said.

Then he did. It was a squeak, a training shoe on the rain-slicked pavement.

Somebody was coming, walking fast. Deegan looked agitated.

'Tony, that you?'

Aidan saw a figure emerge from the darkness. Raindrops sparkled around the outline. The man was too short, too thin to be Tony. The driver was one of those steroid men. The stranger at the end of the street pointed something.

'Aidan,' Deegan yelled as he shifted from anxiety to action. 'Get in the car!'

Aidan felt himself being bundled into the BMW. He tried to look round but Deegan shoved his head down. Before Aidan could protest the night roared and the rear windscreen shattered. Glass showered him followed by stinging rain. Suddenly his blood was on fire and the whole world was swimming before his eyes.

'Stay down,' Deegan yelled.

He reached for the keys. There were running feet, then the sound of the ignition. Before Aidan could draw breath two things happened: the driver's side window exploded and the engine revved into life. His pulse was jumping. They were being shot at. The car leapt forward and he heard a heavy thud, their attacker trying to cling on and failing.

'What are you doing?' Aidan yelled. 'Let me out. This doesn't have anything to do with me.'

Terror flooded through him.

'Shut up and stay the hell down,' Deegan snapped.

In spite of everything that had happened he sounded in control. Aidan did as he was told. Behind him he could hear voices fading into the pounding rain. One of them belonged to Mum. She was calling his name.

Ten minutes later they stopped. Every nerve was still jangling. Aidan was shaking, not sure whether he would be able to stand. Imaginary shots were crashing in his ears. Deegan got out of the car. He seemed so cool. He was fiddling with a bunch of keys. Aidan rose shakily to his feet and looked around.

'Where are we?' he asked. 'Who was that shooting at you?'

'Shut up and sit tight,' Deegan told him.

Voice measured and calm, he was in control. Scared as Aidan was he managed a protest.

'Stop telling me to shut up.'

Deegan pointed a thick finger but he didn't speak. The finger said: Shut up. He released a heavy padlock and swung open a steel gate. It was a second hand motor dealership. Ninety seconds later he drove out in a Ford Focus.

'Get in,' he said.

Aidan's mind flickered. Options, what were his options?

'No way,' he said, edging away. 'It's stolen.'

'It's not stolen,' Deegan said. 'It's back up. Now get in.'

But Aidan wanted answers.

'What happened back there?'

As if he didn't already know. 'Somebody tried to kill me,' Deegan said. 'Now get in the car.'

Aidan shook his head.

'You can do what you like,' Aidan said. 'Leave me out of it.'

Deegan got out and dragged him towards the car by a fistful of drenched sleeve. Aidan struggled.

'Get off me! All anybody ever does is shove me around.'

His words had no effect on Deegan. The pushing continued. Aidan felt his arm slam against metal and he winced.

'Do as you're told,' Deegan warned.

There wasn't much choice. Seconds later they were gunning down the empty road in the direction of the Pier Head. Aidan was nursing his sore arm. Oblivious, Deegan hung a left.

'Where are we going?' Aidan asked.

'Tunnel.'

Panic rose in his throat

'Oh no. You're not taking me with you.'

Somehow, leaving Liverpool would be like closing a door. Everything he knew would be on the other side. His hand moved instinctively toward the door handle.

'I'm not going with you. You can't make me.'

He grabbed the handle.

'Don't even think about it,' said Deegan.

As if making his point he accelerated hard and Liverpool flashed by. Aidan's heart was pumping fast.

'Listen,' he said. 'You don't need me. Let me out.'

Deegan shook his head. 'I can't spare the time.'

His face twisted. The tunnel swallowed them.

'Now . . .'

His knuckles whitened. Helpless as he was scared, Aidan admitted defeat.

'I know,' he said, breath shuddering out of him. 'Shut up.'

PART TWO
Light in a dark room

One

The ring tone of a mobile phone shrilled in a Glasgow flat. A balding man in his late thirties picked it up.

'Yes, this is Alex McLeish. Mr Geraghty? Good to hear from you. I've been expecting your call. You find my terms suitable then?'

McLeish glanced at his wife and mouthed the word: pen. She gave a disapproving look and opened a drawer. Taking the notepad and biro from her, he walked out onto the balcony cradling the phone under his chin.

'Tomorrow?'

He let the caller wait a few moments. An old tactic. Make them wait, then reel them in. 'It's short notice but I think I could do that.'

He noticed his wife watching and turned away. He knew that scowl of old. Why the sour face? Couldn't she just accept that this was what he did for a living?

'I'll be coming by rail,' he said. 'Can you get somebody to meet me?'

He scribbled a name and number on the pad.

'OK, I'll give him a call. Good to speak to you, Mr . . .'

But Geraghty had already hung up. McLeish shook his head. Wouldn't hurt to show some manners, would it? He punched in the phone number he had been given. Somebody answered right away.

'Steve. This is Alex. Yes, the Scotsman. That's a sharp ear you've got, Scouse. Can't pull the wool over your eyes, can I?' McLeish listened for a moment.

'That'll do nicely. Keep it somewhere safe and we can pick it up when I arrive.'

The voice at the other end crackled for a moment.

'No probs. I'll get in touch with the station and call you back.'

'You don't call the local station any more,' his wife said from the living room. 'You're living in the past, Alex. They have a national help line.'

'I know how to get the train times,' McLeish snapped. 'Anyway, I thought I told you not to earwig on my business.'

She looked at him for a moment then used the remote control to turn up the volume on the TV. It was a *Columbo* re-run. She liked Columbo. You could rely on him. More than could be said of her husband.

McLeish got the train time and phoned Steve back.

'Aye, twelve o'clock,' he said, before quipping: 'Carry a bunch of red roses.'

Steve laughed.

'See you tomorrow,' McLeish said.

Then, ending the call, he looked across the grey, innercity district and added:

'High noon.'

Two

The hillside froze in a flash of lightning.

They were only an hour, maybe an hour and a half, from Liverpool but the world couldn't be more different. The houses and flats, the traffic, the streetlights, the whole relentless rush of the city had given way to the lowering solitude of rural north Wales.

'Now what?' Aidan asked.

He looked out of the rain-spattered window and saw the massive stillness of the mountains.

'We can't just sit here all night.'

They'd pulled into a long, unmarked lane and were parked among the trees. Deegan had killed the headlights before turning. From time to time the wind blew strongly and the leaves unburdened themselves of torrents of rain-water that drummed deafeningly on the roof.

'Did you hear me?' Aidan said. 'We can't . . .'

Deegan shot out a finger.

'Don't you tell me what I can or can't do. Just button it and let me think.'

The air was turning cool. Aidan's top was stained dark with the rain and it was making him uncomfortable. He looked for something to wrap round his shoulders. No luck. He stole a glance at Deegan. The man in black looked strained. Aidan had almost started feeling sorry for him when Deegan reached out his hand.

'Mobile,' he said.

'What?'

'Give me your mobile.'

'I haven't got one,' Aidan told him.

'Don't give me that,' Deegan snapped. 'Everybody has a mobile.'

'No, I mean I have but it's in my room. I don't have anything on me.'

Theatrically, Aidan pulled out his pockets.

'See, no phone, no money, nothing. You can check if you like.'

Maybe that's what a man like you does, Aidan thought bitterly. You pat down your son for hidden phones and bugs.

Deegan stared at him for a moment then his eyes moved away.

'I just want to make sure you don't contact anybody,' he said. 'Stay here. I'm going to make a call.'

He paused before adding:

'And no funny business.'

Aidan's heart jumped. For a moment he actually thought Deegan was going to a phone box. That would give him time to get away, find a house from which he could call home, the police even. He had no great plan, just wishful thinking. But at least there was hope of a kind. Disappointment followed immediately. It was a dumb idea. Why would he bother with a phone box? Talk about clutching at straws. What Deegan meant was he was stepping out of earshot. He walked as far as a five-barred gate and pulled out a mobile. He made three phone calls in quick succession. The third seemed to make him angry and he started kicking the gate and cursing.

'Right,' Deegan said on his return, 'Here's what we're going to do. It's half past two in the morning, too late to go knocking at a B&B. We're going to get our heads down here tonight.'

'You're off your head,' Aidan protested. 'I'm not sleeping in a car. I want to go home.'

Deegan chuckled. 'Tell me something,' he said. 'When did I say this was a democracy? If I say we sleep in the car, we sleep in the car. Do I make myself clear?'

'But what do you want me for?' Aidan cried. 'What's the point of all this?'

Deegan's eyes swivelled in his direction.

'Do you understand what happened tonight?' he said. 'Somebody tried to shoot me.'

He made a gun with his finger and thumb.

'He didn't care if you got in the way either. Liverpool isn't safe, not for me, not for you, not till I get this sorted. Until I do . . .'

He flipped a switch under the dashboard and the boot popped open.

'Until I do we stay put.'

Aidan tried to argue back. He wanted to tell Deegan he was being stupid, that what he'd said made no sense, but he wasn't listening. Deegan walked round the back of the car and returned with a couple of blankets. Aidan got an idea that there was planning in this. The way the car had been ready in the lock-up, the way Deegan had this stuff stashed in the boot, he'd left nothing to chance. He'd been expecting an attack.

'Wrap yourself up in that,' Deegan said. 'And don't say another word until I give you the green light.'

Aidan went to answer back but Deegan gave him a look that said: *don't you dare*.

This time Aidan did as he was told.

When Aidan woke there was a sour taste in his mouth. His stomach griped. Worse, there was a sense of hopelessness grinding through his insides. He couldn't tell if Deegan was awake. He had his back to Aidan. He'd slept in the driver's seat. Wondering what time it was, Aidan sat up. Immediately Deegan spun round. 'What are you up to?'

'I was only trying to find out the time,' Aidan answered acidly. 'I'm cold, I'm hungry and I want to know the time. Is that a crime?'

Deegan ignored the question.

'It's half past seven.'

'I've got to phone Mum,' Aidan said.

Then, seeing the look on Deegan's face he added the magic word.

'Please.'

Deegan thought for a moment then produced his mobile.

'Just one thing,' he said. 'You keep it short and sweet. You tell her you're all right . . . and you hang up.'

'But she'll want to know what's going on,' Aidan said.

'Tough,' said Deegan. 'She's probably got the police round by now. We do it my way or we don't do it at all. Now stop going on. I've got to let the dust settle. Just give me time and I'll work out a way to get you home.'

'OK,' Aidan said, discouraged.

Deegan handed him the phone and he punched in the number. Mum came on the line.

'Aidan! Where are you? We've been worried sick.'

'I'm OK, Mum. There's no need to worry.'

Her words came tumbling out. Aidan had never heard her sounding so desperate.

'But where are you? When's he bringing you back? Put Sean on.'

Deegan snatched the phone out of his hand. Without a word he ended the call.

'That'll do,' he said.

Before Aidan could say a thing Deegan got out of the car and smashed the handset against a tree. 'What the hell are you doing?' Aidan cried.

He stared at the pieces scattered on the ground.

'Oh, that's just great,' he cried. 'What if she wants to phone me back?'

'Sorry,' Deegan said. 'But that isn't an option.'

'And if I want to call her again?'

'This is how I operate,' Deegan said, pulling a couple more mobiles from his pocket. 'I change phones all the time. That way nobody can trace me. Behave yourself and you can make another call later.'

That was it, conversation over. He stretched then climbed into the driver's seat and gestured to Aidan to join him in the front. Deegan's gaze wandered the farm buildings that squatted in the murk at the end of the lane.

'First things first,' he said. 'Breakfast.'

Aidan wasn't arguing. That was what the sour taste was. He was starving. They drove to a Little Chef tucked in behind a crossroads. Deegan prowled round the car park for a while, clocking the number plates and scanning the main road, before waving Aidan out of the car. Sure, Aidan thought, like there would be some psycho checking every Little Chef in a hundred mile radius. At the door Deegan gripped his arm.

'You want to eat, don't you?'

'Of course.'

'Then act normal. We're just a dad and his son having a bite to eat.'

Just a dad and his son? Don't make me laugh, Aidan thought. We're an accident of biology, not a relationship.

'Sure, whatever.'

Deegan picked up a complimentary copy of the *Daily Mail* and pointed Aidan in the direction of a table. Aidan was going to make a crack, ask him if he needed help with the big words. Then he remembered his run-in with Paul Gorman and thought better of it. A big mouth is a mouth that gets filled in. They sat in the far corner of the restaurant. Aidan knew what that was about. Deegan wanted to see who came in and who went out. Talk about paranoia.

'We made the paper,' he said.

He shoved the *Mail* across the table. The story was four lines in a news round-up column.

'It doesn't mention either of us,' Aidan said. 'Just the shooting.'

The waitress was making her way towards them. Deegan gestured for Aidan to be quiet. They ordered full English breakfasts. As Aidan gratefully forked down bacon and egg he remembered the morning in the supermarket cafe. It seemed a long time ago.

'I like this,' Deegan said.

'The breakfast?'

'The freedom,' he explained. 'Out on the road. Nothing to tie you down.'

'When do I get to go home?' Aidan asked, keeping his voice low so he didn't make Deegan angry.

'Soon as I can. I need to make sure it's safe first.'

'Why can't you just leave me at a station somewhere?' Aidan said. 'Give me the train fare and I'll make my own way back. What have you got to screw my life up for? This doesn't have anything to do with me.'

'You're my son so it's got everything to do with you. You might not think that way but my enemies do.'

Aidan felt the same shudder of revulsion. Whatever he was to Deegan, he wasn't his son, not in the way most people understand the word. 'They wouldn't come after me for that,' he said. 'You don't mean anything to me. What makes you think they'd come after me?'

'The people we're dealing with don't leave loose ends,' Deegan said, taking a swallow of hot, sweet tea.

Aidan listened, then shook his head. He had a feeling there was a wider agenda.

'I've had enough. You can't hold me against my will.'

'I can do what I want,' Deegan said. 'I'll tell you when it's safe to go home.'

'That's not fair!'

An elderly couple looked in their direction. Deegan leaned closer. His eyes were white-hot pokers searing into Aidan.

'Don't do that again.'

An hour later they were sitting in a lay-by. Aidan was a prisoner. Why was Deegan doing this?

'What now?' Aidan asked.

Deegan held up his hand and carried on reading the paper. He'd just bought it from a newsagent next to the Little Chef. It was the *Daily Post*. It served Merseyside and North Wales and he thought it would carry more detail than the nationals. Aidan tried a different question.

'What does it say?'

'Not much. The police are playing their cards close to their chests. You're a complication. Maybe they want to keep your name out of the papers.'

'Why?'

He shrugged.

'Who understands coppers?'

'But why would they want to keep my name out of the news?' Aidan asked. 'Surely they'll be making an appeal or something.'

'Not if they think it will spook me,' Deegan said. 'By now they'll know I'm your dad. Maybe they think that counts for something.'

Aidan caught his eye.

'Does it?'

'What do you think?'

Aidan gave a little shake of the head, a small gesture that stood for a lot of anger. Typical of Deegan to answer a question with a question.

'Count?' Aidan said. 'It didn't for fifteen years.'

'Fifteen?' Deegan said. 'You've got your maths wrong there, lad. More like thirteen, twelve even.'

Aidan did a double-take.

'What are you on about?'

Deegan turned his eyes on Aidan.

'Sounds like Jill didn't tell you everything, after all. I can't blame her. She doesn't want me messing up her cosy, middle-class life, does she? She always had big ideas, did Jill. One time I missed getting arrested by this much.'

He gestured with thumb and finger.

'So when I get home Jill greets me with a paint chart in her hand. Look, I'll give you the unauthorised version, Aidan, the bit your mother didn't tell you, what some people call the truth. I was still in your life when you were little. Maybe you've got me down as some kind of low life but I didn't just walk away the moment you were born. Believe me, I stayed around. I was a proper dad, at least at first. I heard your first words, saw your first steps.' He rummaged in his pocket and produced two crumpled photos. One showed Deegan cradling a baby. To Aidan, the kid looked like a pink turnip. It could have been anybody. The second clinched it. The beaming toddler sitting on Deegan's shoulders was unmistakeably him.

'There's the proof,' Deegan said. 'Some things you can't erase.'

Aidan couldn't handle it. So he wasn't a baby when he left Liverpool. He was eighteen months, possibly two years old. He'd had a life with this man. For however short a time, Deegan had been a father to him. So why couldn't Aidan remember him? Do little kids forget that quickly? Deegan took back the photos.

'Convinced?'

Aidan nodded, but it didn't change anything.

'Look, this doesn't have anything to do with me,' he said. 'Why don't you . . . ?'

'Don't ask me to drop you at the station again,' Deegan said. 'It isn't going to happen.'

'So what is?'

Deegan folded the paper and consulted a road map.

'I came here a couple of times when I was a kid,' he said. 'Mrs Evans will put us up.'

'Who's Mrs Evans?' Aidan asked.

'She runs a B&B. We had a few days holiday in Rhyl when I was a nipper. It was about the happiest time of my life.'

Wonderful, Aidan thought, first he decides to rediscover what it's like to be a dad, now he wants to relive his own childhood. On their way to Rhyl Deegan laid out the ground rules. Aidan was to act normal. For some reason Deegan was big on normal, which seemed a bit rich in his line of work. Aidan was to speak when spoken to. Most of all, there was to be no funny business, no running off, no trying to call Mum. Deegan asked Aidan if he got it. Aidan said he did. Then he tried to say something else. Guess what, Deegan told him to shut up.

Deegan was in for a disappointment at Mrs Evans' B&B.

The sign over the door said it belonged to Mr and Mrs Williams.

'What happened to Mrs Evans?' Deegan asked when they got inside.

'Oh, that's my mum,' said Mrs Williams. 'Have you stayed here before?'

There was something in her look.

'Yes,' Deegan said. 'When I was a kid.'

Mrs Williams looked at him with interest.

'I would have been around then. I can't be much older than you.'

Deegan frowned for a moment then his eyes lit up.

'You must be Ceri.'

'That's right. You've got a good memory.'

Deegan grinned.

'No wonder. I fancied you rotten at the time.'

Mrs Williams pulled a face. Talk about striking a false note.

'What's the name?' she asked.

Deegan delivered the false name without hesitation.

'Sean Flaherty.'

Aidan recognised Deegan's sister's married name.

'Your rooms are upstairs to the left,' said Mrs Williams, handing over the keys.

'What happened to your mum?' Deegan asked.

Mrs Williams' voice dulled. 'She's in a nursing home. She had a stroke. I'm afraid she's never been the same since.'

Deegan looked genuinely upset.

'I'm sorry to hear that,' he said. 'She's a lovely lady.'

Mrs Williams nodded. Aidan was glad to walk away from the uncomfortable silence that followed.

'So what was that about?' he asked.

Deegan had pushed him into the first room and closed the door.

'I told you. I was happy here. Mrs Evans is one of the few people who was ever nice to me.'

Aidan mimicked playing a violin. 'Aw diddums,' he said, suddenly emboldened. 'Just a victim, aren't you? You had a lousy life so you had no choice but to deal drugs. You're pathetic, you know that?'

Deegan's eyes flashed fire.

'What do you know, Aidan? I bet you've never gone short of anything. You've never had to scrape for a living.'

Self-pity turned to anger in an instant.

'You think you know me?' he snarled. 'You think you can look down your nose at me?'

He came across like somebody out of *The Sopranos*, but Aidan wasn't about to tell him that. His eyes radiated anger.

'You think you know where I'm coming from? How could you, Little Lord Suburban Spoilt Brat? I'll tell you what makes me tick. The way my life was, I was at the bottom of the food chain. One day I decided to move up.' Aidan wasn't coming out with flip comments now. The way the veins swelled in Deegan's face, the way he leaned forward taut as a coiled spring, he had Aidan's attention all right.

'You know what Darwinism is?' he said.

Hey, Aidan thought, big word for a thug.

'I think so. Survival of the fittest, right?'

'Got it in one.'

Deegan's hands closed into fists.

'Survival of the fittest, that's the name of the game. You can put a suit on a man, scrub him up as clean as you like, but if he comes from the streets you'll never wash away the dark inside. He's fought for his little scrap of turf all his life. He's done things that make him sick to the pit of his stomach. Me, I don't try to wash anything away. I don't feel regret. I'm never guilty. What's the point? I accept my darkness.'

Aidan's face rumpled into a sceptical frown but he said nothing.

'You can't even imagine what makes me tick,' Deegan went on. 'I saw a documentary once. Do you know the toughest survivor on the planet? It's the cockroach. Cool customer, Mr Cockroach. He can even survive a nuclear explosion. All that radiation just bounces off his shiny little shell. He's a born fighter. He'll get down as dirty as you like, just so long as he makes it.'

A cockroach, Aidan thought, well you certainly aimed high in life! He kept it to himself. He was mouthy, not suicidal.

'Don't make fun of me, Aidan,' Deegan said, pulling out a roll of cash. 'See this? There's more here than your old fella earns in a couple of months, posh as he is. I've got the cars. I've got a villa in Spain. I can have a different woman every night. I'll go to a club and buy four or five bottles of champagne at £50 a throw.' He flashed his watch.

'See this? It's a Rolex. £25K to you. You know I was even thinking of buying a helicopter once,' he went on, spit spraying from his lips. 'Not bad for a snotty-nosed kid from the back streets of Liverpool. Old Joe Kenny, he worked his guts out for over forty years and you know what he got for it, a lousy pension and a body eaten away by cancer. That was never going to be me. Like I said, I started life at the bottom of the food chain . . .'

He shoved his face into Aidan's.

'The point is: I didn't stay there.'

Three

While Deegan was having his say, plans were being laid elsewhere. In a hotel suite in Liverpool city centre, a meeting was about to take place behind closed doors. A tall, greying half-skeleton of a man was sitting at a round table, eyes fixed on, but not looking at, a picture on the wall. Ten years in prison had withered him. He was toying with a bottle of Budweiser. His name was Dave Geraghty. There was a knock at the door. He glanced at a burly minder.

'That'll be him.'

The minder opened the door and stepped back.

'Come in . . .'

Before Geraghty could say another word, the newcomer interrupted.

'No names,' he said. 'You can call me the Gunslinger.'

The minder started to laugh. The look the Gunslinger gave him killed the sound in his throat.

'What's up?' Geraghty asked. 'Are you worried about listening devices? Do you really think I'm trying to fit you up?'

'Right now I don't think anything,' the Gunslinger said. 'I just don't want you using my name.'

'Fair enough,' said Geraghty. 'I'm pretty big on security myself.'

The Gunslinger didn't answer. Instead he took a seat, yawned and said:

'I did everything you asked. The intelligence was good. Your man fouled up.'

'You're right,' said Geraghty. 'He talked a good fight. I won't be using him again.'

'No?'

'No. I'm ready for Plan B.'

The Gunslinger gave a half-smile.

'That right? How do you know where he is?'

He didn't say Deegan but they both knew who he meant.

'I don't. That's why you're here. Can you find him?'

The Gunslinger looked around the room.

'It shouldn't be a problem. What's it worth?'

Geraghty shoved a note across the table. A sequence of numbers was written on it.

'Your fee.'

The Gunslinger read it, then tore it into bits.

'Hang on there,' Geraghty said. 'That's a generous offer.'

The Gunslinger smiled.

'I didn't say it wasn't.'

The Gunslinger wrote down an address. Geraghty read it and frowned.

'Rhyl. What's he doing there, topping up his tan?'

'Call it a sentimental journey.'

Geraghty stared.

'We are talking about the same Sean Deegan?'

'That's right. Same one that blew away the back of your Carl's head, if I remember.'

He waited a beat to let it sink in.

'Same one that got you sent down for a stretch the same year.'

Geraghty's face twitched. He didn't need reminding that

he'd spent nearly half his adult life inside. He'd always been cock of the prison wing but he had two craft-knife scars on his stomach to show for it. It was a few moments before he waved the piece of paper. 'You're sure about this?'

'I'm sure.'

Geraghty nodded.

'Nice one.'

He tossed a fat envelope across the table. The Gunslinger picked it up and walked briskly to the door. There was no need to count the money.

'By the way,' Geraghty asked. 'Why the Gunslinger?'

'Don't read much, do you?'

Geraghty pulled a face.

'What's that got to do with anything?'

'Read the right books and you'd know.'

Four

It took Aidan an hour to pluck up the courage to protest.

'I hope you don't expect me to sit around here all day.'

He was trying to do defiance. All he could manage was a petulant bleat. Deegan ignored him at first. He just stared at the TV screen. A chef was making something delicious from pasta, garlic, tomatoes and anchovies.

'Did you hear me?' Aidan said, frustration putting a touch of steel in to his voice.

'Why can't I go to my own room? You did pay for two, you know.'

Finally, Deegan turned.

'That's right. I paid for two.'

'So why can't I . . . ?'

'What do you think? It was only for appearances, so Mrs Williams doesn't get suspicious.'

His eyes went back to the TV screen.

'But if you imagine you'll be leaving my sight then you're living in a dream world. I wasn't born yesterday, Aidan. You'd do a runner as soon as look.'

'So this is it?' Aidan said. 'You won't let me go home. You won't let me phone Mum. I'm supposed to sit here in limbo. This is crazy. What's it all about?'

Deegan fired off a one-word answer:

'Survival.'

It didn't stop Aidan having another go.

'I'm bored. I'm fed up.'

He left out the most important complaint: I'm scared. He knew that wouldn't cut much ice with Deegan. Giving it one last try, Aidan tugged at his tee-shirt. 'And I stink.'

Now he had Deegan's attention. It was something he'd been at pains to make clear: appearances matter. You are what you wear, what you drive, who you own. Deegan examined Aidan. The rain from the night before had left a stain around the upper arms and shoulders.

'OK,' he said. 'We're going out. But remember . . .'

'Yeah, yeah,' Aidan said. 'I know. No funny business.'

First stop was a sports shop. They wandered the aisles for a few minutes. Aidan saw an Ellesse dress and thought about Jade. Trouble is, he also thought about Paul Gorman and his flesh crawled. Deegan saw him looking at the dress and frowned. 'What are you doing?' he said. 'I thought you were getting some clothes.'

Aidan nodded and moved on. While he picked his gear Deegan watched from behind Gucci sunglasses. Aidan guessed he had to be into *The Matrix* or Tarantino. His nose wrinkled. Woof rotten woof, we're a pair of *Reservoir Dogs*.

'What's up?' Aidan asked, looking at the trackie and top. 'Too expensive?'

'Joking, aren't you?'

'This is all Nike and Adidas. What's wrong with it?'

Deegan shrugged.

'Aren't you getting anything?' Aidan asked.

Deegan chose quickly.

'Looks like I'll have to,' he said. 'I don't think I'll have much choice out here.'

He made Rhyl sound like one of the moons of Jupiter, not a seaside town in North Wales.

'Come on,' he said, darting a look at the CCTV cameras. 'Let's pay.' The shop assistant stared when Deegan rolled a handful of notes off his wad of cash. Noticing the reaction, Deegan smiled. He might be on the run but he was still putting on a show. It wasn't completely lost on Aidan. He didn't like Deegan, but he couldn't help thinking about what he had. It's the dream, isn't it, all the money you need, nobody to boss you round.

'I don't go in for plastic,' Deegan said.

They talked on the way back. Aidan knew he wasn't getting the whole truth. It was obvious he meant something to Deegan though. At least, he had once. Then something happened. Deegan didn't get round to saying what. His mobile rang. Aidan was getting used to the routine. There would be snatched conversations, frowns, sharp words. One name he heard again and again was Tony.

'He's my *consigliore*.' Deegan said.

'*Consigliore*?' Aidan asked.

'Haven't you ever seen *The Godfather*?' Deegan said.

'Of course I have,' Aidan said. 'One, two and three, if you must know. I do a mean Robert De Niro.'

'Then you should know what I'm talking about. It's Mafia-speak. The *consigliore* is the Don's right hand man.'

Aidan rolled his eyes.

'And you think you're *the Don*?'

Deegan actually looked slightly embarrassed.

'I'm what I want to be, soft lad.' So that was Tony. He was Deegan's driver, his right-hand man, his lieutenant. From the look on Deegan's face, this time the *consigliore* had bad news. Aidan shot him a question.

'Something wrong?'

They were heading back to the B&B along the Promenade. Deegan frowned the question away and made another call. Aidan watched him pacing up and down with his mobile pressed to his ear.

'Are you going to tell me?' he said.

'It's nothing,' Deegan told him.

'You're getting pretty agitated over nothing,' Aidan observed.

'You really want to know?' Deegan said. 'You want to know what's upsetting me? It's just the little matter of somebody trying to top me. They've got somebody in, a Scotsman called the Gunslinger. A Glasgow boy.'

'You're joking, right?'

Aidan knew his Stephen King. He'd read *Wizard and Glass* a month or two earlier.

He and Chris had been on one of their horror and fantasy binges at the time, a feast of six hundred page novels and computer games.

'Do you see me laughing?' Deegan said. 'I know Glasgow well. If I give it some thought I might just put a face to this Gunslinger. I tell you, it's a tough town. These boys mean business.'

'It just sounds so corny,' Aidan said. 'How do you know you can believe this Tony anyway?'

'Are you trying to be funny?' Deegan said. 'If he says this character's blown into town, then that's what's happened. Tony and me, we grew up together. We're blood brothers. I've known him since I was five years old. If I can't trust him, I can't trust anybody. We started out selling £10 wraps together. He watched my back. I watched his. We clawed our way up together. Even when I was out in Spain Tony never once thought of taking over the business for himself. If I'd asked anybody else to stand in for me, they'd have taken the lot. That kind of loyalty you can't buy. It comes from in here.'

He put a hand to his heart.

'£10 wraps?' Aidan asked. 'You mean drugs, don't you?'

'Grow up,' Deegan said. 'Of course I mean drugs. As long as people want to shove stuff in their arm or push it up their nose, as long as there's demand, there's going to be a supplier.'

It was always there, what he did for a living.

'Don't think you can judge me,' he said. 'Get real, lad, the illegal drugs trade is one of the world's key industries. We're talking nearly ten per cent of the global economy. They don't tell you that in school, do they? Ooh, those terrible drugs, just say no. What they don't say is, those magic little substances make the world go round. When I was growing up, it was a clear choice, drugs or the dole.'

'Don't give me that,' Aidan said. 'You're just making excuses for yourself. It wasn't the only way.'

A moment's thought, then:

'You could have tried getting an education, for starters.'

Listen to me, Aidan thought, I'm starting to sound like Mark. The three Rs: read, write and get rich.

Deegan's lips curled, half smile, half snarl.

'You're joking, right?

'No.'

Deegan didn't try to explain himself. He just shook his head as if Aidan had suggested he become a female impersonator. He rolled his sleeves up and showed Aidan his forearms.

'See any marks? I don't do smack, I don't even smoke pot. You know what, you might not believe me but I've never even touched a cigarette. I'm not putting any of that rubbish in my body. What do you think I am, some kind of moron? As far as I'm concerned it's a business. Some company director sells weapons abroad, and they blow a kid's legs off, I don't see him getting locked up. No, they give him a knighthood. Services to the economy. Same with booze and ciggies. They do more damage than crack or heroin put together. People don't get sent to jail for opening an off-licence though, do they? Listen here, Aidan, if some loser wants to poison himself that's his problem.'

Rolling the sleeves back down, he looked at Aidan.

'I mean, do you think I'm stupid? You know why I do it? Simple, it's the best business on Earth, pure capitalism. People need a fix. I provide it. It makes me a good living. Money, girls, power – you can have the lot, and you can have it quick. Your Daddy doesn't have to be rich. It's a level playing field, real democracy. If you're hard enough, you're good enough. You've just got to be able to handle yourself.'

'So you're proud of what you do?' Aidan said.

'I'm not ashamed of it,' Deegan answered, his voice even. 'You want rules? I've got loads. I make them up as I go along. Whatever I want is right. How about that for a rulebook, Aidan?'

Aidan got up and started walking.

'It's not mine,' Aidan told him.

'That's your choice,' Deegan said. 'But you'll never understand me until you understand the drug. You know what the drug is? The drug is the buzz. The drug is pain and relief from pain. The drug is hell and the promise of heaven. The drug is a wad of cash and the hole in your pocket. The drug is business, lad, the drug is life.'

Aidan stared in disbelief. Could this piece of crap really be his dad?

'Anyway,' Deegan said. 'Here endeth the lesson. Let's go eat.'

*

They sat in the corner of McDonald's. Aidan watched Deegan eating, his jaws clicking. He couldn't get what Deegan said out of his mind. Suddenly he was torn with guilt that he hadn't tried harder to get away. He knew, first chance he got, he was going to run.

'I'm going for a Jimmy,' Deegan said, standing up.

Aidan looked away.

'Suit yourself.'

Deegan didn't tell Aidan to go with him. Aidan stared in disbelief. I don't believe it, you think you've won me over. The moment the door closed behind Deegan, Aidan was on his feet. Well, think again! Snatching the change from the meal that Deegan had left on the table, he raced across the road and down a side-street. There was only one thing on his mind: escape. He could hear his feet pounding on the pavement, his breath coming in gasps. Not once did he look back. That would just be tempting providence. Finally, he stopped an elderly couple.

'Phone box,' he panted. 'Could you direct me to a phone box?'

He found it two streets away.

'Mum?'

'Aidan, thank God. Where are you?'

'Rhyl. Yes, of course the one in North Wales.'

What a stupid question!

'I got away from him. Look, I haven't got much money, a bit of loose change, that's all. Can you come for me?'

Hope crept into Mum's voice.

'Of course I will. Listen Aidan, there's a policeman here. I want you to talk to him.'

Aidan heard the man's voice.

'Are you on your own, Aidan?'

'Yes.'

'Where's Deegan?'

Aidan looked up and down the street.

'I don't know. I gave him the slip.'

'So he's still around?'

Instinctively, Aidan looked around him.

'Yes.'

'OK, give me the location of the phone box. I'll get the local police to come for you. But if you see Deegan and you have to move, you've got to try to find the nearest police station. Can you do that?'

'I'll try.'

'Where were you when you last saw Deegan?'

Aidan froze. Getting away from him was one thing, grassing him up was another.

'A few streets away,' he said. 'I don't know what it's called.'

He didn't mention McDonald's. There were other questions. He answered in monosyllables. Disappointed, the policeman finally handed the phone back to Mum.

'My money's running out,' Aidan said.

'Try to stay calm,' Mum said, her voice shaking. 'Just come home, Aidan. I love you.'

The phone went dead.

'Yes,' Aidan said to nobody. 'I love you too.'

Five

It was hard to know what to do. Aidan felt lost. Should he stand outside and wait for the police? That seemed to make sense, but what about Deegan? He'd be out of McDonald's and scouring the streets by now. I'd just be making it easy for him, Aidan thought. He'd see me for sure. Somehow Aidan couldn't think clearly. Anxiety was throbbing through his system like an electric charge. He just wanted the police to come. Why didn't they come?

Aidan darted a hopeful look along the street but there was no sign of the police. All he could see was an old man walking his dog. Why didn't they come? His mind raced. Had he said the phone number right? One wrong digit and he was stuffed. Could they have gone to the wrong call box? He started to think about making his way to the police station. For a moment his mind was made up. Yes, he would go to the police station. His resolve didn't last long. He imagined Deegan round one of those street corners and the thought just bled away.

He stayed in the phone box and waited.

A few miles away, a silver Honda Accord turned off the A55. At the wheel was a specimen of Kirkdale-born muscle called Steve Jones. In the passenger seat sat the balding

Scot, Alex McLeish. They didn't speak. Jones was busy clocking the road signs. McLeish was checking his weapon, a Tokarev semi-automatic pistol. They were taking a roundabout when McLeish's mobile rang.

'Yes?'

It was Geraghty asking where they were.

'Rhyl just coming up.'

He glanced at Jones.

'Four miles?' he asked.

Jones raised three fingers. McLeish relayed the information.

'The job's as good as done.'

Aidan chanced another glance along the street and his heart jolted. Deegan. Aidan's lips sagged open. His pulse leapt in his throat.

Where were the police?

About the same time the question strobed through his mind, Deegan saw him. The expressionless eyes leapt with recognition. The world seemed to tilt and whirl. Aidan threw open the phone box door and ran. Deegan came after him. Thick-set as he was, there wasn't much fat on him. He was solid rather than heavy, and he worked out. Aidan caught sight of himself in a shop window. His face, his eyes, his mouth were wild with fright. Aidan saw Deegan coming closer and he knew he wasn't going to get away. He turned to face Deegan, instinctively cowering under his anger.

'What do you think you're doing?' Deegan hissed, seizing Aidan by the wrist. 'This isn't a game, you know.'

He glanced back at the phone box.

'Did you make a call?'

He read Aidan's eyes.

'You did, didn't you? Who was it? Who did you call?'

'Mum.'

It was as if Aidan had thrown a bone to a mad dog. Deegan wanted more.

'And?'

'And what?'

'What about the police? Were they with her?'

Aidan nodded.

'Oh, that's just dandy, that is,' Deegan groaned, stepping back. 'Do you understand what you've done?'

Suddenly Aidan found the strength to fight back. Deegan had no right to shove him around.

'I told them to come and get me,' Aidan snapped. 'What's wrong with that?'

'Nothing,' Deegan said, 'So long as you don't mind going home in a box.'

'What are you talking about?'

'You really think you can trust the coppers? Forget *The Bill* and the stuff you see on TV. This is the real world. Your friendly boys in blue live by the same rules as the villains. Do you think they really keep their noses clean and wait for their pension? Of course not, they're flesh and blood like you and me, always on the look-out for a scam. They steal half the gear that comes into the station and sell it back to the street. You think putting a uniform on somebody's back makes them straight? Dream on. For every one who wants to fight the bad guys there's another who'd sell his own mother for a couple of hundred quid.'

'I don't believe you,' Aidan said.

He wondered if Deegan was telling the truth, or just acting the big man. It all sounded too much like a bad movie to be real. Deegan stabbed a finger at Aidan.

'I should know what I'm talking about. I've bought more coppers than you've had hot dinners. So has Geraghty.'

'Who?'

Aidan seemed to know the name, but he wasn't sure where he'd heard it.

'Dave Geraghty,' Deegan answered. Something between caution and puzzlement came into his face. His tone softened.

'Are you being straight with me, Aidan? You don't recognise the name?'

Then Aidan's eyes lit. It had come back to him. Jade had told him about Geraghty but he shook his head all the same. The ground was giving way beneath him.

'Well, this is a turn up,' Deegan said. 'I thought you knew.'

Pandora's Box was open and Deegan didn't plan to close it again.

'Geraghty's the one who ordered the hit. It was revenge for what I did to his kid brother.'

He paused to study Aidan's expression.

'You're sure you don't know?'

Aidan did now. Deegan had filled in the gaps in Jade's knowledge. Believing Aidan's story, Deegan pulled a face.

'And I thought Jill had told you everything.'

Something was surfacing. An image filled Aidan's mind: a white figure crucified on a cross of flame. Then more: Mum's face, and words, her words.

Look what you've done.

Oh, good God Almighty, Sean, look what you've done.

Aidan reeled from the memory flash.

Sean, look what you've done.

. . . Sean . . .

'It was you,' Aidan said, his voice barely rising above a whisper. 'It's you in my dream. You killed that man. I was there when you did it.'

Deegan looked back at him.

'Yes, I killed him.'

At last Aidan understood. His life made sense.

Ten minutes later they were sitting side by side in a seafront shelter looking out at the grey waves. They'd ducked inside to avoid the police cars that were cruising the streets. Aidan wondered at his own reaction. He should have been screaming, trying to break away from Deegan. Instead he was calm. He was finding out where he'd come from.

'You killed a man.'

It was a statement, not a question. Deegan nodded.

'Yes.'

'How do you live with that?'

Deegan took another glance round the corner of the shelter. Reassured that the police had gone he answered.

'He was going to kill me. Two men went into a house. Only one was going to come out. I made sure it was me.'

He had a way of punching out his answers. They were simple, unambiguous and savage.

'I told you before,' he said. 'Survival of the fittest.'

But Aidan was hardly listening to him. He'd moved on. What bothered him now was Mum and how she had lied to him. One thing mattered more than any other – the reason they had had to leave Liverpool – and she had left it out completely. What else was she hiding? Suddenly home didn't seem so wonderful. Aidan was confused. To be honest, he didn't care whether the police came or not. OK, so being with Deegan wasn't his idea of fun, listening to him talk about his sick, brutal world, but he had no place he would rather be. In his own way, Deegan did seem to care. Aidan stared at the horizon and he felt empty. 'What a mess,' he said.

'It can be cleared up.'

'How?' Aidan said. 'Who are you going to kill this time?'

Deegan just looked ahead.

'Go on, tell me, how is it going to be cleared up?'

'You don't need to know.'

'Don't I? You made me watch a man die. I was only two.'

Deegan shifted his weight and turned to face Aidan.

'You weren't meant to be there. You saw me go into the house. I didn't know you were there, either of you.'

'And that makes it better, I suppose? My dad can be a murderer, just so long as I don't know.'

Aidan stood up.

'Great logic. You know what, you should have written sorry letters for Jack the Ripper.'

'Sit down, Aidan.'

'Why the hell should I?'

Deegan planted his hands on his knees. It was a deliberate gesture; he was losing patience.

'Because the coppers are looking for me. Most of all, because I told you to.'

Exasperated, Aidan threw a punch at him. He parried it.

'Want to land one on your old man?' he said, standing up and waving Aidan forward.

'Go on, try it. Land one on me and I'll drive you anywhere you like.'

'Don't be stupid.'

Without warning, Deegan shot out a jab that made Aidan's ears ring. 'Hit me,' he said.

Aidan did as he was told, or tried to. He came at Deegan, swinging. Deegan slapped his punches away as if they were nothing.

'Is that all you've got?' he asked. 'You hit like a girl.'

He meant it as a joke, but it stung. Aidan put everything

133

into one last right-hander. Deegan feinted and stabbed a straight right into Aidan's face. Aidan staggered back, his eyes smarting. Deegan probably pulled the punch but it hurt like hell.

'Are you crying?' Deegan asked.

'No!'

'You are, aren't you?'

Deegan dropped his hands.

'You'll never make a fighter,' he said.

That's when all the rage and resentment boiled up in Aidan. He lashed out with his fist and felt Deegan's nose crunch. Deegan stared in surprise for a moment and wiped away a slight trickle of blood. Then he laughed.

'A bit of a foul blow,' he said. 'But who said you had to play fair? Nice one, son.'

Aidan couldn't believe it. He'd hit Deegan and it made the moron proud as punch!

'You can drop the act,' Aidan told him. 'You're not really my dad. You're nothing, just an accident of history.'

'Yes,' Deegan said, hurt showing in his voice. 'That's about right, an accident of history.'

He lowered himself back onto the bench and Aidan looked down at him. He seemed suddenly tired.

'You look like you've given up,' Aidan said.

'You're not far wrong,' Deegan said. 'I feel like throwing my hand in, all right.' He produced his mobile.

'I've done nothing but call people. You know what, none of them want to know. Suddenly I'm a leper. I'm starting to think I made a big mistake. You know why I'm here? I came back from Spain to take back my turf. I've been on the run since I hit Carl Geraghty.'

'So why come back?'

'Why do you think?' Deegan said. 'I'm running out of money. It seems times have moved on. I'm a dinosaur at

34. But for Tony, I'd be on my own. Tony's done his best, but he doesn't have my rep. He couldn't stop guys bailing. It's Dave Geraghty, he's the problem. I got him sent down for a ten year stretch. Since he came out of prison, he's been taking over my territory. Men I made out of nothing have gone over to him.'

'Hang on,' Aidan said. 'What do you mean, you got this Geraghty sent down?'

'When I whacked his kid brother, he came looking for me. It wasn't me he found. He got Jimmy Gorman.'

The name sent a shudder through Aidan. Could this be a coincidence?

'Gorman? Did he have a son called Paul?'

'That's right. I think you saw me with him.'

'Yes, you handed him something. Drugs?'

Deegan shook his head.

'Money for his old lady. I owe her for what happened to Jimmy. Anyway, Tony and me always ran things together. Jimmy was younger. He hung around with us. He wanted to be one of the big boys, make it the Three Musketeers. He never had much nous but we used him as muscle. Then Dave Geraghty got hold of him.'

'He killed him?'

Deegan nodded.

'Yes, soon as he'd had his fun.'

For once Deegan showed his feelings. His face was lined with guilt.

'So how did you get Geraghty sent to prison? Wasn't he going down for killing Gorman anyway?'

Deegan shook his head.

'There was no evidence. Men like Geraghty, they know how to work the system. Only Tony and me, we worked it better. We arranged some evidence of our own. Remember what I said about bent coppers?'

Aidan stared back.

'I called in a favour from your friendly neighbourhood crooked CID. That's how Geraghty got sent down. Now he's out and he's hungry.'

Deegan took a long, troubled breath.

'I haven't fought hard enough for what's mine. Tony ran things for years but he can't cope. Geraghty is taking over, bleeding me dry. That's why I came back, to plug the holes in my operation. Tony didn't like it at first but he knows his place. He was never going to be more than a stop-gap. Not as it's done much good, me coming back. Looks like I'm too late to make any difference. I'm finished, Aidan. I'm just about on my own.'

Aidan should have walked away but for some reason he actually felt sorry for Deegan.

'So go back to Spain.'

'And do what? Work in a bar? Sit rotting on the Costa Brava? When I had money and power I was somebody, Aidan. The story is as old as time. The warrior takes the spoils. I can't go back to the way I was, a nobody.'

Aidan listened to the seagulls keening overhead. 'It's better than winding up dead.'

Deegan cracked his knuckles.

'You sure about that?'

He started talking about his life: driving through Liverpool at high speed with the lights off, haggling with the Turks, the Colombians, going over to the Dam to do a deal . . .

'The Dam?'

'Amsterdam.'

He talked about it all: the days when the dealers sold their wraps from behind an iron door and the times they used Bearcat scanning devices to intercept police frequencies. He gave it all a kind of murky glamour. Or tried. Aidan's face betrayed his feelings.

'Do you think I'm trying to make it sound exciting?' Deegan said. 'Do you think I'm trying to recruit you to a life of crime?'

'Aren't you?'

He shrugged the question away.

'One thing's for sure,' he said. 'I don't want that life for you. Your mum's done all right.'

This was a turn up for the books, a kind word for Mum.

'You're not like me, lad. You don't have to beat the system. They've trained you to make your way inside it. You can have anything you want: nice house, nice car, wife, kids, and all legit. You've got a future.'

'You know something,' Aidan said. 'I don't understand you at all. One minute you're going on about how you're this great survivor, as if it's some really big deal, the next you're telling me to stick with what I've got.'

Deegan didn't answer. Instead, he gave Aidan a dig in the ribs. 'Cop car,' he said. 'We've got to move.'

Six

Less than an hour later they were driving out of town in a second hand Scorpio. Deegan had paid cash and Aidan didn't notice any documents being exchanged. It was as if he lived in a completely different world where the wheeler-dealer was King.

'I don't get it,' Aidan said. 'Is there a kind of villains' *Yellow Pages*?'

'You could say that,' Deegan said. 'But there's no hard copy. It's all in here.'

The usual touch to the forehead.

'I recognise this road,' Aidan said, changing the subject.

'You should,' said Deegan. 'It leads to Mrs Williams' B&B then out to the A55. I'm taking you home.'

'Home? You mean back to Liverpool?'

Deegan nodded.

'I was stupid and selfish to keep you with me. I just wanted . . .'

He met Aidan's eyes.

'I've made a real mess of things. Crazy as it may sound, I wanted to be your dad.'

'What's this?' Aidan said. 'Midlife crisis. You want to get in touch with your feminine side.'

'You calling me gay?' Deegan asked, genuinely offended.

Cockroach he could take. Gay? Now that was one step too far.

'Forget it,' Aidan said, musing over the twisted logic. 'Just my sense of humour.'

He saw that Deegan wasn't slowing down.

'Aren't we going to call in for our stuff?' Aidan asked.

Deegan shook his head. 'We can replace it. There's no point taking risks. The coppers might have found the B&B.'

'How could they?'

Deegan shrugged.

'It depends how much Jill's told them. I must have mentioned the holiday to her sometime. You tell your woman most things.'

Aidan didn't like the way he called Mum *his woman*.

'How's she going to remember something like that?' Aidan said. 'It's over ten years since you've seen each other.'

'Can't be too careful,' said Deegan.

Even that didn't make any sense. They were hardly being cautious, driving past the top of Mrs Williams' road. Aidan had a feeling he wanted to see the place one more time, before he said goodbye to that last little scrap of childhood. But this one reckless act was going to cost him dear. They were coasting past Mrs Williams' road when Aidan saw a silver car pull up at the Give Way sign. He met the driver's eyes.

In the silver Honda, Jones and McLeish exchanged glances.

'You're sure that's them?' asked Jones, releasing the handbrake.

McLeish nodded.

'It's them. I think the kid might have clocked us though.'

'You sure?'

'No, not sure. It's just a feeling.'

Jones allowed an elderly couple in a Ford Fiesta to get between the Scorpio and himself, then pulled out on to the main road.

'I like facts, not feelings,' he said. 'Let's see if they try to shake us off.'

Aidan had a feeling too. He glanced in the wing mirror then craned his neck to look back at the Honda.

'What's up?' Deegan asked.

'That Honda,' Aidan said. 'The silver one. I could have sworn one of the men looked at me.'

Deegan wrinkled his nose.

'Sounds like paranoia to me, Aidan.'

He didn't dismiss it, though. He too looked back, searching for faces in his rear-view mirror.

'I can't make much out,' he said. 'There's a car in the way. What makes you think this fellow was looking at you?'

'It's hard to put my finger on it,' Aidan said. 'It's just . . .'

He tried to explain.

'Look, you know when you catch somebody's eye?'

Deegan gave a twitch of the head, something less than a nod.

'Usually they look away. This man, he kind of leaned forward.'

Aidan dropped back in the passenger seat.

'Oh, I don't know. It could only have been a split second. Maybe I am paranoid.'

Deegan's eyes darted back at the rear-view mirror.

'Trust your instincts,' he said. 'They're right as often as they're wrong.'

Aidan thought he was trying to sound streetwise. He just came across dumb. Half the time you're right, half the time you're wrong. Great odds. Deegan put his foot down on the accelerator and took another look in the mirror.

'You could be right,' he said.

'What do you mean?'

'He's moved out to get past the Fiesta. Could be he's just an impatient driver. Let's put him to the test.'

They had reached a roundabout. It was signposted Rhuddlan Castle to the left. Deegan indicated right. In the wing mirror Aidan saw the Honda follow suit. Then he understood what Deegan was up to. He went twice round the roundabout. The Honda followed, doing both circuits.

'OK,' Deegan said. 'That seals it. We're being followed.'

In the Honda McLeish cursed.

'Well done, Steve. You just fell for the oldest trick in the book. Now he's onto us.'

'So he's onto us,' Jones said. 'It isn't going to do him much good.'

He accelerated, closing the gap on the Scorpio. McLeish pulled out his mobile and phoned Geraghty.

'Mr Geraghty? Yes, it's me. We've picked up Deegan. He's seen us.'

He pulled the phone away from his ear and glanced at Jones, screwing up his face.

'Listen boss, there's nothing we could do about it. It wasn't Deegan rumbled us. It was the kid. Yes, I know, it's just one of those things.'

Geraghty's impatience came crackling through the voice piece.

'The job's going to get done, OK. We're not going to lose him.'

Geraghty's voice crackled again and McLeish answered.

'Yes, that's a promise.'

*

The world was ripping open at the seams. Aidan had been on his way home. Now this.

'What are we going to do?' he said.

Deegan's face was unreadable.

'Well?'

'We're going to get out of it.'

He was trying to reassure Aidan. It wasn't working.

'Really?' Aidan cried. 'And how are we going to do that?'

Deegan waited for the speed limit to change then accelerated hard and pulled away.

'Are they following?' Aidan asked.

'Oh, they're following, all right,' Deegan said, checking the rear-view mirror.

'Aren't you scared?' Aidan demanded. 'Those men want to kill you.'

'Correct,' said Deegan. 'They want to kill me. They would probably kill you too, as a witness. Well, here's a promise, Aidan. I will protect you, no matter what it takes. They've just stepped on to my patch. We're going to be all right.'

Somehow Aidan believed him. In one way, he was a monster. But Aidan knew Deegan would do anything to keep him safe. In the wing mirror he saw the Honda coming up fast.

'He's gaining on you.'

'He can do what he wants. I'm not trying to outrun him. I couldn't if I wanted. He's got the newer engine. Plus the North Wales police are keen as mustard on speeding.'

'So what are you doing?' Aidan asked.

'Simple,' Deegan said. 'I'm taking him where I want to go. My place, my time . . .'

He flipped the catch to the glove compartment. The moment Aidan saw the revolver a plug of fear clogged his throat. Deegan smiled and finished the sentence:

'My tools.'

They drove through Denbigh and out into the countryside. Deegan didn't say much. He drove at an even speed, checking the mirror from time to time.

'Good game, cat and mouse,' he said. 'I just wonder how sharp his claws are.'

'How can you be so cool about this?' Aidan said.

'Just in case you haven't noticed,' Deegan retorted. 'I don't have a choice. It was Dave Geraghty's call. He's the one who declared war. This is the next battle.'

Aidan watched the hills flashing past.

'How can you live like this?' he asked.

'I'm not that different to anyone else,' Deegan said. 'Your mum knew what I was like. I told her what I was into but she stayed for the ride. She had plenty of opportunities to walk away. She didn't, not until . . .'

'Until you killed Carl Geraghty.'

'Yes.'

A moment of silence, then:

'But they're no better than me, any of them. You think your Granddad's a great man, don't you?'

'I think he's a good man.'

'Yes? Well, let me tell you about good old Joe Kenny. I was in love with your mum. Yes, that's right, really in love – hearts, flowers, the whole deal. I didn't just get her up the duff. Whatever the Kennys have said to poison you against me, that's not the way it was. I was a kid, not much older than you, just seventeen years old when we met. Sure, I was a bit of a scally, but nothing heavy when I first started going out with Jill. I'd have jacked it all in for her, got a lousy nine-to-five, gone straight. She mattered that much. Joe never gave me a chance though.'

Aidan wasn't having it.

'Maybe he could see how you were going to turn out.'

Deegan pulled a face.

'I can't say I ever saw him with a crystal ball in his hand. No, Joe Kenny didn't give me a chance. He wasn't always the walking corpse he is now. He really laid into me. He hurt me the way nobody's ever hurt me before or since. He just balled his fist and drove it into the pit of my stomach. No warning. He wasn't having some two-bit scally ruining his daughter's life, that's what he said. I was on my knees gasping for air when he booted me in the ribs. He broke two of them. He even stamped on my hand when I was trying to get up. A real humanitarian, old Joe.'

Deegan's eyes nailed Aidan.

'He left me bleeding on the floor. I was screaming, begging him to stop. Yes, good old Joe, pillar of the community, he beat a seventeen-year-old lad to a pulp.'

Aidan noticed that the speedo had touched seventy. Deegan took the hint and eased off the gas.

'If he'd given me a chance, things could have been different. Everything could have been different.'

Aidan didn't know what to make of it. Stumped for something to say, he noted:

'They're still behind us.'

'I know,' said Deegan. 'That's where I want them, for now.'

Jones guided the car along the narrow, winding road, squinting against the strong sunlight that lanced through the lattice-work of branches overhead.

'Where the hell's he going?' he said. 'Doesn't he know this is exactly the kind of out-of-the way place we're looking for?'

McLeish was feeling uncomfortable too. In ten years at this dangerous game, nobody had ever strung him along like this. Deegan had the kid with him and he was behaving as though he didn't have a care in the world. He seemed to be playing into their hands. But why would he? All of a sudden, fragments of the street myths Geraghty had told about Deegan came sluttering into his mind. In a dangerous world, their prey had survived a long time. No, professional that he was, McLeish didn't like this at all.

'Keep your eyes on the car,' he said. 'He's got to be up to something.'

That's when Jones swung round a sharp bend and hissed through his teeth. A van was coming in the opposite direction. There was no room for two cars to pass. He slammed on the brakes. As the car rocked to a halt he smashed the heel of his hand into the steering wheel. Cursing loudly, he let the oncoming vehicle pass and accelerated after Deegan.

'Where is he?'

Jones's eyes raked the road ahead.

'I can't see him.'

The Honda's engine whined as it climbed the steep gradient.

'Go back,' said McLeish. 'We'd have spotted him by now.'

He was right. The road climbed in front of them in a more or less straight line. It was empty.

Unclipping his seatbelt, Jones twisted round and reversed at speed.

'There!' shouted McLeish. They'd just driven past a concealed path that wound into thick woods. Jones pulled on the handbrake, put the car into first and swung it on to the rutted, potholed track.

'How did we miss it?' he snapped.

'What does it matter?' McLeish barked back. 'So long as we find him.'

Aidan saw the Honda approaching, flashing in the tree-filtered sunlight. Crouching behind a mouldy tree trunk, he breathed noisily through his mouth. Anxious, tense with fright, he was in a kind of blood fever. He watched the car bumping over the uneven road and his heart quickened. He pulled shallow breaths into his lungs and waited. The car was almost level with him, huddled in the hiding place Deegan had given him. Against Deegan's orders, Aidan chanced a glance over the trunk. Suddenly Deegan reversed out of the gloom of the woods, spinning tyres throwing up leaf mould, and slammed the boot of the Scorpio into the Honda's front wing. Two heads pitched forward and the airbags detonated. Deegan moved fast. His powerful form seemed to blur, silhouetted against the sunlight, as he went to the car. Seeing him moving like that, assured and in command, Aidan felt his fear drain away. Wrenching open the driver's door, Deegan pistol-whipped the driver. Tendrils of bright scarlet blood spread across the man's face. Something about the set of Deegan's expression said he was about to finish the job.

'No!'

The cry burst from Aidan. Shame burned in his cheeks, shame for the man who was his father, shame at his collusion in the attack. Part of him knew it had to be like this but the raw, primal violence sickened him to his stomach. Deegan was taking him beyond the limits of civilised behaviour. He had the gun trained on the passenger's head. He was made for this moment. 'Get out!' he ordered.

The man did as he was told. He was still raising his hands to his head when Deegan kicked him to the ground. The kneeling man's face was pinched and white. Aidan could tell, even from this distance, that he was trembling. He was expecting the worst.

'Here,' Deegan said, calling Aidan from the woods.

He had a screwdriver. Aidan questioned him with his eyes.

'Do the tyres.'

Aidan walked round the car punching the screwdriver into the rubber. Satisfied, Deegan looked at the passenger.

'Are you the Gunslinger?' he asked.

Aidan saw the puzzled frown. Deegan rewarded it with a savage back-handed slap to the cheek.

'Don't come the innocent with me,' he snarled. 'I know what's going down. Scottish accent, Tokarev pistol in the car. I was warned about you, scumbag. Are you the Gunslinger?'

'I don't know what you're talking about.'

Deegan drew his arm back again.

'No!' Aidan cried, the second time he had objected.

Then:

'Please.'

Deegan put the gun to McLeish's knee. Aidan looked away.

'Last chance, are you the Gunslinger?'

A shake of the head.

'You lie and you don't walk again.'

Then, in a voice filled with terror, the words of admission poured out. 'OK, OK, I'm the Gunslinger. Just don't do my knees. I'm the Gunslinger, the tag they give me back home.'

McLeish's eyes were wide with fear.

'That's what you want to hear, right?'

There was a look of satisfaction from Deegan:

'Him?'

A nod in the direction of the senseless driver.

'Jones.'

'Is he another Jock?'

McLeish shook his head.

'I'm the only one from Glasgow. They wanted an out-of-towner for the job. He's local, one of Geraghty's. About as much use as a pair of wooden underpants.'

'Who put you onto me?' Deegan demanded. 'How did you know where I was?' He mentioned a name from CID, the bent copper he'd been going on about.

'Never heard of him,' said McLeish.

He grimaced, anticipating another blow.

'I told you, I'm from out of town. How would I know the local filth?'

Deegan seemed to accept this. He had examined McLeish's expression and he trusted his own instincts. It was the truth.

'What are you going to do with them?' Aidan asked, dreading the answer.

Deegan considered for a moment.

'Do me a favour,' he said. 'There are some ties on the back seat.'

'Ties?'

'Yes, plastic ties. You get them from Garden Centres. They use them to put round plants and trees.'

Shocked as Aidan was by the brutality of the last few minutes, he couldn't help but marvel at Deegan's organisation. It was like Batman's utility belt. He seemed to have prepared for any eventuality. Aidan found the ties in a hurry and handed them to Deegan. He was still worried Deegan might top the pair of them, the Jock and the Scouser. Deegan used the ties to secure first McLeish's hands, then the unconscious Jones's. Finally, popping the Honda's bonnet, he ripped out a couple of cables and tossed them into the woods.

'They won't be going far for a while,' he said, satisfied. 'Let's move.'

*

It was a while before Aidan realised where they were. Exhausted, or maybe just wanting to shut out the murky world into which he had slipped, he had fallen asleep.

'Where are we?' he said, sitting up and noticing that they were in a built-up area.

Deegan swung round a bend and they were facing the Overhead Railway. They were back in Elmwood Street. It was late evening. The sky had clouded over and a fine drizzle was falling. Aidan breathed deeply. Could it really be over?

'You'd better get indoors before somebody spots us,' Deegan said.

'What about you?' Aidan said.

'What about me?'

'What are you going to do now?'

'Maybe I'll go back to Spain after all,' he said, scanning the street. 'There are worse things than running a bar.'

'You telling me you can walk away that easily?'

'I don't have much choice, Aidan. Me and Tony against the numbers Geraghty can put on the street? I waited too long before I came back.'

'Look, Aidan,' he went on. 'There's no need for speeches. I do care about you. I wish things had turned out differently.'

Aidan was halfway out of the car when he hesitated.

'Just one thing,' he said. 'You know the way you go on about all the women you've had?'

'Yes?'

'You must have other kids. I bet you have.'

Deegan didn't deny it.

'So?'

'Why the big interest in me, then? Why'm I so special? What's all this about?'

Deegan took a while to answer.

'You might be clever,' he said wearily. 'Book clever, but you're not that sharp, are you?'

Aidan frowned.

'What are you getting at?'

'It's your mum,' Deegan said. 'She's the only woman I ever cared about. I never felt that way with anybody else. Yes, even men like me have feelings. With all the others it was just . . . physical. I was scratching an itch. Jill, I could have had a life with her, with both of you. She really meant something. First time in my life I had a real family . . .'

He shook his head. ' . . . And I made a mess of it. The day I killed Carl Geraghty I killed my chances with you and your mum. When I got involved in the business I thought I could earn some money and get out. It doesn't work like that. These things have a habit of taking over.'

Aidan stood by the car.

'See you,' he said.

'Yes, see you, son.'

With that, Deegan drove away.

Seven

Aidan walked up to the house just as the darkness thickened into night. The drizzle had become a steady downpour. Wet streaks cut through the grime on window panes like cracks in an old oil painting. The top of the street disappeared behind a cage of rain and mist.

As Aidan hovered in front of number 66 his head was pounding with exhaustion. Then a thought crawled into his brain: how do I pick my life up again? What do I say to Mum? Then more thoughts bubbled up. There would be interviews with the police, questions, recriminations. Was he ready for this? He was beyond alone. Here, in the blackness, he could feel his life stripped down to the bone. For a moment he even thought about walking away again, where to he didn't really know. Now he understood the attraction of all those movies where the hero walks off into the distance, destination unknown. He didn't walk away. He was no hero. He just stood there, wet, uncertain, more a piece of street furniture than a human being. Somebody must have seen him from the window because Mum came flying to the door.

'Aidan!'

She ran out into the street and threw her arms around him. Tears started in his eyes.

He hugged back then remembered the things Deegan had said and stiffened at the press of her body. She immediately sensed his coldness and took a step back, her hands resting on his upper arms. He saw Dad and Gran hovering in the lighted doorway, reluctant to intrude.

'Oh God, Aidan,' Mum said. 'You don't know how scared I've been.'

She looked up the street.

'Where's Sean?'

A man Aidan didn't know had pushed between Dad and Gran. A policeman, had to be.

'He's gone.'

Mum nodded.

'Are you OK?'

'Of course I am. He wouldn't hurt me.'

Aidan surprised himself with the words. Since when did he feel anything for Sean Deegan? Since when did he owe him any loyalty?

'He shouldn't have taken you away,' Mum said. 'He had no right.'

A reply forced its way to Aidan's lips, simple but loaded with meaning.

'He's my father.'

The skin pulled tight over Mum's cheekbones. Relieved as she was, she wasn't going to take this lying down.

'Your dad is standing right there,' she said, pointing at Mark.

'Yes,' Aidan said. 'I know, but Sean Deegan is my father. It's a fact of life.'

Aidan sensed the policeman's presence and looked in his direction. Mum introduced them. Aidan didn't register the rank.

'Sorry, what did you say?'

'I'm Inspector Johnson,' said the policeman. 'We need to talk. Tomorrow will do. Unless you'd like—'

'Tomorrow,' Aidan said.

Johnson glanced at Mum.

'Tomorrow it is then,' he said. 'Say eleven o'clock.'

'That'll be fine,' Mum told him, an unmistakeable note of dismissal in her voice. 'Thanks for everything.' Aidan wasn't quite sure why she was thanking Johnson. Aidan was the one who'd given Deegan the slip. He'd called home. All the police had done was fail to turn up at the phone box in time. In the end, of course, it was Deegan himself who'd finished the whole episode, disarming those men, bringing him back home. His son, his choice.

'Let's go inside, Aidan,' Mum said.

Aidan let himself be guided into the house. He wanted Mum's arms round him but there was something in the way. He knew things that put a wall between them. Aidan listened to the voices booming around him, saw their faces as if in a dream. Yet it all seemed so very far away, unreal. He was back, with Mum and Dad, Gran and Granddad. He was in a family. But it was like those seaside holiday cut-outs, where you stick your head through the hole and make yourself look like a strongman or a cartoon mouse. Mum, Dad, his grandparents, they weren't really there. Where the real people were meant to be there were just holes. Where his family was meant to be there was emptiness.

Inspector Johnson was punctual. By five past eleven next morning they were sitting in the kitchen. There were four of them: Aidan, Mum, Johnson, and a policewoman by the name of Corvin or Carvin. Dad stayed out of it. He said they were going home in a couple of days, once Aidan had had a chance to get over his ordeal. That's what Dad called it: Aidan's *ordeal*. Strange as it may seem, that's not how it felt to Aidan. Yes, he'd been frightened, he'd been mad as a sewer rat too, but he'd learned something. He'd got to know himself and that he could be just that little bit better. That was down to Deegan. Aidan didn't know if he liked him all that much, and he certainly didn't admire him, but he'd begun to understand him. There had been a meeting of minds, of sorts. Deegan was part of what Aidan was. Gran, of course, was flitting around in the shadows, ready to serve drinks and snacks. The adults already had coffees. Aidan nursed a can of Diet Coke.

'I want you to tell me what happened, Aidan,' Johnson said, 'from start to finish if you don't mind. Anytime you get tired or want a break, just say.'

'He didn't kidnap me,' Aidan said. 'He just wanted me out of harm's way. You know that, don't you?'

'That's as may be,' said Johnson, exchanging glances with Mum. 'But just tell me what happened, step by step.'

'I will,' Aidan said. 'But you have to understand. OK, so I haven't seen him since I was a little kid, but he is my father. He wouldn't do anything to hurt me. You do believe me, don't you? He didn't do anything wrong.'

Mum put her hand on Aidan's arm. He couldn't help flinching. She took the hint and pulled away. Johnson noticed. So did the policewoman.

'It's Geraghty you should be interviewing. He's the one who sent the gunman after us that night.'

Aidan was careful to say gun*man*. He didn't want to let slip about the two men in the woods and what Deegan had done to them. That would be harder to explain. The myth of Deegan as no more than an over-zealous father would fall apart in an instant. Johnson held up his hand.

'Look, I respect your loyalty, Aidan, but let's stick to the facts. There's no point making allegations against Mr

Geraghty. That's hearsay. All I want in your statement is a factual explanation of what happened to you.'

'But Sean Deegan, my father, he'll be all right, won't he?' Aidan asked. 'You won't put him away.'

'If he hasn't done anything wrong,' Johnson said, 'then he's in the clear. OK son, just the facts now, off you go.'

So Aidan talked: about the attempted shooting, the drive through the tunnel, the B&B. He told them about the way he tried to get away. He left out the incident with Jones and McLeish. He wasn't going to tell them anything that showed Deegan in a poor light.

'Can we go back to yesterday?' Johnson said, reading over his notes. 'You were with him quite a while after that first attempt at escape. Why didn't you try to get away again, call for help, anything?'

Aidan saw Mum looking. How could he tell the truth, that it was because of her, that after what Deegan told him, for a while he hardly cared whether he came home again or not?

'I . . . In the end I got to . . .'

'Yes?'

With Mum watching him he felt uncomfortable. The skin on his back prickled.

'Look, you might not understand this. I mean, you've got him down as a thug, a gangster, I don't know what.'

Aidan was floundering. He didn't know what he wanted to say himself.

'There's more to him than that,' Aidan managed at long last. 'By the end, I got to trust him.'

Johnson gave him a look that said: *whatever rings your bell*. Mum just seemed to shrink away from him. Aidan was relieved when the whole thing was over.

'So what are you going to do?' he said.

Johnson slipped on his coat.

'In what way?'

'About Deegan.'

'If everything you say here is true,' he said, tapping his notebook, 'then Mr Deegan has done nothing wrong. He could have been more considerate to your mother, but I don't believe he has committed an offence. Your mum doesn't want to make a complaint.'

He glanced at her.

'Do you, Mrs Shaw?'

Mum shook her head.

'That's it then.'

Gran showed the two officers to the door. Mum sat next to Aidan, not saying a word.

'Are you upset?' she asked.

'No, not really.'

'I said I trusted him.'

'And that's the truth?'

Aidan searched his mind for the answer.

'It probably sounds crazy,' he said, 'but yes, yes it is.'

'And me?' Mum said. 'Do you trust me?'

Aidan pushed back his chair and walked to the door.

'We can talk later,' he said. 'I'm going to find Jade.'

For once, Jade was home. Mrs Harding let Aidan in. The house was tidier. Not tidy – there was still the overwhelming stench of cat and tobacco – but it was a big improvement on his previous visit.

'Jade,' Mrs Harding called up the stairs. 'Somebody to see you.' Aidan heard footsteps, then Jade appeared at the top of the stairs. She was wearing blue-black jeans with a broad leather belt and a black tee-shirt. She raced halfway down, face flushed, then she stopped for some reason and the smile fell away. Aidan was disappointed she hadn't kept on going. He wanted to touch her. He wondered what was holding her back – her mother's presence maybe – but there was something else. He could sense the space between them.

'I heard you were back,' she said. 'Are you OK?'

Her voice was flat. Tiny strings of hope snapped inside him. What was the matter with her? Surely they had more than this.

'Yes,' Aidan said. 'I'm fine.'

Jade looked different. Her face was pale and pinched. Though her hair was scraped back from her face, strands hung loose. This girl, who had always tried to act so cool, who had always been so immaculate in her appearance, was flustered and tense, even more vulnerable than he'd remembered. What disturbed him most was that some of the life seemed to have gone out of her. Ever so slowly, struggling for the words, she started to speak.

'It must have been . . .'

Aidan interrupted her.

'It was. Can we talk about something else, at least for now?'

Can we talk about us, is what he wanted to say. Will you let me put right all that stuff about Emily? Jade continued down the stairs and led him into the living room. He felt it again, the distance.

'You've had a tidy-up,' he said, glancing round.

Uncomfortable wasn't the word for the way he was feeling. Something had changed. Was it Jade or was it him?

'Yes,' Jade said. 'It was Mum's idea. She's making an effort. We're going to decorate.'

Aidan had the strangest feeling, as if they were skating on a frozen pond, skirting the centre where it thinned dangerously. They seemed to have come to an unspoken agreement: that it was best to talk about absolutely nothing.

'So what's been happening while I was away?'

Jade shifted uncomfortably from one foot to the other.

'Nothing,' she said. 'You're the one who's had all the excitement.'

'Yes, I suppose so.'

This wasn't going the way he'd been expecting. He'd expected closeness, the meeting of hearts and minds towards which they'd been edging before he went. All they had now was a big, fat zero, the embarrassed mumblings of near-strangers. Aidan glanced at his watch.

'Look, I'd better be going. There's lots of stuff to sort out before I go home.'

Jade's eyes flashed.

'Home? When do you leave?'

'Not sure yet,' he said. 'It'll be tomorrow or the day after. We haven't really talked about it yet. Everything's been . . . weird.'

'You'll come round, won't you, before you go? You'll remember to say goodbye.'

'Of course.'

Aidan let himself out, but as he crossed the street he felt as if they'd done it already, they'd said goodbye.

Fielding questions from Mum and Gran, Aidan retreated upstairs to his room. He didn't want to talk. There was a ball of disappointment in his throat and his eyes were stinging. There was a time Jade had wanted reassurance from him. Now the boot was on the other foot. He lay on his back and stared at the ceiling, as derelict and empty as he had ever been in his life. The ceiling was pale like Jade's face and as colourless as the conversation they'd just had. He couldn't believe the way things had turned out. He was still nursing his disappointment when there was a knock at the door.

'Is it OK if I come in, Aidan?'

It was Dad.

'Sure, why not?'

Aidan sat up. He leaned against the wall.

'How are you feeling, son?'

He was trying to sound casual but the way he said that last little three-letter word made them both self-conscious.

'It came as a bit of a shock, I suppose, finding out the way you did.'

'Yes.'

'Your mum had her reasons, you know. When you were little, you wouldn't have understood. Later . . . well, it just got difficult. There was no easy way to tell you. It isn't easy to admit mistakes to your kids. You're meant to be there for them, strong, the one with all the answers. Besides, Deegan was gone, gone for good we thought. Why rake up the past? There didn't seem much point.'

'There's always the truth,' Aidan said.

He didn't want this conversation. He didn't want to talk. He didn't want to listen.

What he wanted was Jade, the Jade he'd held and begun to . . . No, not that word, not love, not now it had died.

'Yes,' Dad said. 'There's always the truth.'

He looked down into the street.

'You're still my son,' he said. 'Nothing's changed there.'

'I know.'

Aidan had been waiting for something like this. It was always going to be a matter of going through the motions. Nothing Mum or Dad could say was going to make him feel any better. He knew all about his past, but that was Deegan's doing, not theirs. What was the point of going into all the whys and wherefores? Who wants to pick at a sore? On past performance, Mum and Dad were never going to be particularly honest about it anyway.

'When do we go home?' Aidan asked.

Dad hesitated. There was obviously a lot more he wanted to say, but he seemed to have decided this wasn't the time.

'Tomorrow,' he said. 'If the police need us again, they can phone us at home. There doesn't seem much point hanging round here.'

He must have remembered Granddad, because he added:

'Your mum will be popping up regularly to see how Joe is.'

Aidan nodded.

'One last thing,' Dad said. 'Did Deegan tell you what his plans were?'

Aidan shrank away from the question.

'Why do you ask?'

'I don't know. Can you imagine how long I've dreaded something like this? I want to be sure he's out of our lives, that's all. For good.'

Aidan got up and headed for the door. 'You don't need to worry, Dad,' he said, stepping out onto the landing. 'He said he was going back to Spain. He's probably already there.'

Dad gave a sigh of relief.

'You won't be seeing him again.'

But Aidan was wrong.

Across town Dave Geraghty was taking stock. Another cock-up. Getting boys to do a man's job. The Jock was a disappointment. He was supposed to be a professional. Geraghty stood up, smoothing his suit trousers. Good thing about Italian, he thought, it doesn't crease. Never lets you down, not like the lame-brains he's got working for him. He walked over to the window. It looked out across the Mersey. He'd bought this riverside penthouse while he was inside. Not like the old days. His dad didn't have a financial advisor to look after things when he was away. That's why the old sod ended up with nothing.

There was a knock at the door.

'Yes?'

'It's me, Dean.'

Dean was the youngest of the Geraghty brothers, twenty years old and itching to prove himself.

'I just heard. Deegan got away again, didn't he?'

'Yes.'

'He's making a fool of us, Dave. Do you want me to go after him?'

Geraghty dismissed the idea with a shake of the head.

'Behave yourself, Dean. I've lost one brother.'

'So what are you going to do, let him walk all over you?'

Geraghty's features hardened. 'It's already taken care of.'

'Meaning?'

'What I say. I always thought it might come down to this. It'll cost but the job will get done.'

Dean frowned.

'You sure?'

Geraghty smiled.

'I'm sure.'

Eight

The bags were in the hallway. It was a done deal. They were going home.

'Care to keep an old man company?' said Granddad, standing at the door to the parlour. He looked like a human pipe cleaner, withered, half-lost in his clothes. Aidan glanced through the living room door at Gran and his parents watching TV and nodded.

'I bet you'll be glad to go home,' Granddad said.

'Not really.'

'How's that?'

'I don't really know,' Aidan said. 'It's like nothing's been sorted out.'

'That's life, Aidan. The ends only get neatly tied up in fairy stories.'

Aidan nodded.

'Yes, maybe.'

Granddad eased himself into his usual chair. Gran hurried from the next room to help him, as if alerted by telepathy. The way she looked at him, the way he squeezed her arm thank you, that was love, as pure, uncomplicated and life-affirming as the dawn light. She lingered a moment then left them alone.

'Deegan's got to you, hasn't he?' Granddad said, checking they couldn't be overheard.

This time, Aidan didn't say anything.

'What's he been saying?'

Aidan came right out with it. He'd never been one to let consequences stand in his way.

'He said nobody ever gave him a chance.'

Granddad threw his head back in exasperation. 'And you swallowed it? That's Deegan all over. He's never done a decent thing in his life, never worked for a living, never lifted a finger to help anybody but himself, never raised a family.'

He sneered at the very thought of the man.

'You know what, he still thinks the world owes him.'

He put on a whining voice.

Nobody loves me. Everybody hates me. I think I'm going to deal drugs. Aidan, the man's no good, never was. The only good thing he ever produced was you.'

Aidan stared straight ahead, not wanting to meet the old man's eyes. Granddad had a gaze that reached right inside you.

'He blamed you,' Aidan said. 'He blamed you for what happened.'

Granddad gripped the armrests. For once the washed-out, yellowish-grey features coloured.

'What!'

'He said you beat him up.'

Granddad slid back in his chair. He was like a boxer rocking back from a punch. 'That's right,' he said at last. 'I gave him a good hiding and I'd do it again if I was strong enough. He was going to drag your mother down, it was obvious. Can you imagine what that's like, watching your child being ruined by some lousy petty villain? Jill was a great kid. She was doing well at school. She had a future and he – that piece of crap – he very nearly destroyed it.'

'He was seventeen, not much older than me.'

'Is that supposed to be an excuse?' Granddad demanded. 'Yes, he was seventeen, but that's where the similarity ends, Aidan. He'd been getting into trouble since he could walk. I'm not saying kids are born evil, but if they're dragged up, if nobody shows them right from wrong, it doesn't take much for them to go off the rails.'

He seemed to chew something over for a moment or two, then he came right out with it:

'I bet he didn't tell you about the old lady he put in hospital.'

It was Aidan's turn to reel from a blow. A shock ran through him, made worse by Mum's appearance at the door.

'No,' Granddad breathed, a cough hacking through him. 'He didn't, did he? He was with another boy, Tony Morrissey, a right animal he was, worse than Deegan if that's possible.'

Tony. Tone. The driver of the blue BMW. Funny how his name kept cropping up. 'It was the eyes you noticed with young Morrissey, hard like stones. He gave me the creeps. I wouldn't put anything past him. I knew he would do somebody damage one day. They worked together, Deegan and Morrissey. Anyway, they came up behind this old dear outside the post office, tried to snatch her purse.'

In his mind's eye, Aidan saw Deegan smiling, heard him talking about the way he'd tried to be a real dad.

'Poor woman,' Granddad continued, shaking his head. 'She hung onto it. So what did Sean Deegan do? He smashed her face into the wall, Aidan, broke her nose, very nearly fractured her skull. That's why I did what I did. I was fighting for your mother's future so I hurt him.

It's the only language he ever understood. That's the way it is when you love somebody. I swear, Aidan, if it would have helped I would have killed him with my bare hands.'

His face was quivering with anger. Rage breathed life into his lined face. In spite of the illness a fire burned in his eyes. 'I'd do it again tomorrow. Believe me, lad, the only thing I regret is that I didn't do a better job, didn't finish the swine.'

It was his turn to notice Mum's presence.

'Sorry love, but it's true. Deegan very nearly ruined your life. Tell the boy. Get him to see through this monster before it's too late.'

Mum glanced at Aidan.

'We'll talk when Aidan feels like listening,' she said.

Granddad wasn't finished yet. He fixed Aidan with a look.

'Make it soon, lad. Listen to your mother, and listen well. You've nothing to learn from Deegan. Nothing!'

With that, he slumped back in his seat.

'Sorry Granddad,' Aidan said. 'I didn't mean to upset you.'

Granddad shook his head. His cheeks were pumping like bellows. Mum took over.

'You didn't upset him, Aidan. It's the thought of what Sean did.'

As Aidan watched Granddad sucking in mouthfuls of air, he wondered where Deegan was, and whether he too was thinking about the past.

It was about eight o'clock when Jade called. Aidan hadn't been expecting it. To be honest, after their uncomfortable meeting that afternoon, he'd decided to try to forget about her. Easier said than done, but when the knock came at the door he didn't expect it to be for him.

'Somebody for you, Aidan,' Gran called.

The dull note in her voice should have alerted him but when he saw who it was he was genuinely surprised.

'Jade!'

'Coming out?'

Aidan gave Gran a sideways glance.

'I won't be long,' he said.

She let her gaze rest on him for a few moments then silently closed the door.

'She doesn't like me, does she?' Jade said.

'You don't always make it easy,' Aidan said.

'Oh, you mean this afternoon?'

'Yes, I mean this afternoon.'

In the quiet that followed Aidan could hear the whisper of the night breeze in the alleys.

'Can we go somewhere?' Jade said. 'There's something I need to tell you.'

Aidan was in no mood for games.

'You can tell me here.'

'No, I can't. We need to be all alone, where nobody is watching or listening.'

A couple of Jade's friends were walking up the street. Did she mean them? It was more likely to be Gran and Granddad.

'Why all the secrecy?' Aidan asked.

A doubt was crawling through the back of his mind. It had always been there.

'Just come with me, will you?' Jade said. 'You'll probably hate me for what I'm going to tell you, but you've got to know.'

The dark smelled of smoke, petrol, dust . . . and fear. They walked as far as a fly-over.

'Where are we going?' Aidan asked.

'There's an island in the middle. It's usually quiet at this time of night.'

They walked through a subway. The walls were alive with spidery graffiti. Yellowish lights burned behind discoloured glass. It was your standard urban nightmare. Jade's traffic island was on the other side of the subway. There was a circular concrete wall, a few boulders and some withered bushes, a council committee's idea of greenery.

'Nice,' Aidan observed caustically.

'We're alone, aren't we?' Jade said. 'Let's sit down.'

She waited for him to join her on the low wall. When he finally sat down he put a little distance between them. The traffic howled on the roadway above.

'OK,' Aidan said. 'I'm all ears.'

'This afternoon I couldn't tell you. The words wouldn't come.'

He stared impassively. He was still listening.

'Are you really telling me you don't have any idea?' she said.

She was aching inside. He half knew what was coming, but he wasn't about to offer a helping hand.

'No,' he said. 'I don't.'

Jade lowered her eyes, shadow falling over her face. However much he'd suspected something, when it came it was a thunderbolt.

'I'm pregnant,' she said.

The night went dead. There was nothing but blank space.

'Aren't you going to say anything?' she asked.

'Is it Paul's?' Aidan said.

She turned to face him. At Paul Gorman's name her eyes clouded.

'Is it?' I repeated.

She nodded.

'When did you know?' he asked.

167

Jade continued to look away.

'Does it matter?'

The blood was roaring in his ears. Was she serious?

'To me it does.'

'Saturday.'

Aidan stood up, fists clenched by his sides.

'The day we went on the ferry?'

'Yes.'

'Oh, brilliant!'

Jade frowned.

'What do you mean?'

'And there was me thinking it was the happiest day of my life.'

Something else occurred to him.

'All that grief you gave me over Emily, and you were—'

Her face hardened.

'I was what?'

'You know.'

'Look, I made a mistake. What right have you got to judge me? It was over before I even met you. It didn't mean anything in the first place. Just a stupid mistake, and anyway, what do I owe you? You weren't bothered about cheating on your own girlfriend. You—'

But Aidan didn't want to hear her. Barely knowing what he was doing, he laced his fingers through her hair and wrenched back her head.

'How could you?' he cried, yelling into her face. 'With him! You're just like your mother, letting yourself be used.'

He saw the startled look in her eyes and let go.

'I'm sorry,' he stammered. I'm sorry. I'd never . . .' She rubbed her scalp. Her eyes were accusing. The anger drained from his voice, replaced by sadness.

'For God's sake, Jade, I cared about you. You're the first one I ever l—'

But Jade wasn't having that.

'Liar!' she spat. 'I was a bit of fun, same way I was for Paul. You're no different.'

Aidan hated her then. He hated her for her fire-flash beauty. He hated her for going with Paul. In his mind's eye, Aidan saw the barbed wire tattoo, the gold ring in his eyebrow. He stumbled back, pointing at her and yelling. Most of all he hated her for seeing through him. The words came out in a stream: cow, bitch and much, much worse. He wanted to hurt her, make her feel the pain that was taking his breath away. Maybe he was looking for an alibi for his own failings. And Jade, she took it all. Her anger shrivelled and she bowed her head. Aidan wasn't calling her anything she hadn't called herself. She needed to be held, to be told she wasn't rubbish. She was scared and miserable and angry with herself, and all he could do was scream and rant and, finally, run away.

She spoke to him because he was the only person who might understand and he left her there, spurned and alone.

Aidan didn't know how long he walked the city streets. Eventually he found a bench where he could see right across the city. There were the Liver Buildings, the Radio City tower, the two cathedrals like ghost ships riding in the mist.

'Jade,' he said, then louder, more accusing: 'Jade, why?'

He was feeling sorry for himself, bitter about Jade, bitter about Mum. The night winds whipped and tore at him but he didn't feel the cold, just the sting of the air in his eyes. It was hard to think beyond Jade's words. She had known. That day on the Mersey, she had known she was carrying

Paul Gorman's child. Suddenly every moment they ever had seemed spoiled, trodden underfoot like rubbish.

'Jade.'

He stayed up there a long time, maybe as much as an hour. He was trudging along the deserted streets when Mum pulled up.

'We've been looking for you everywhere,' she said.

There was relief in her voice but something else too, an accusation. She called home to put everyone's mind at rest.

'OK,' Aidan said. 'Now you've found me.'

'I didn't mean for any of this to turn out the way it has,' Mum said.

'No, I bet you didn't.'

'Don't hate me, Aidan. I chose the wrong man. In spite of everything your grandparents said about Sean, I stuck with him for two years. They were right. I was wrong. I was a fool. Thank God, I saw through him in the end and got away.'

'He says you knew what he was into.'

Mum turned off the engine and twisted to look at him.

'What if I did? I was young. I made excuses for him. It doesn't mean I loved you any less.'

What is it with me? Aidan thought. No matter who he talked to, he was the one who got beaten up.

'I don't know,' he said. 'There's so much to take in.'

He sighed.

'Somehow nothing's as it seems.'

Mum brushed at her sleeve, wiping away something he couldn't see.

'How could you stay with him so long?' he asked, 'knowing what you did?'

Mum hesitated.

'You've been around him,' she said. 'Tell me part of you wasn't won over by him.'

Aidan wanted to protest. He didn't though. She was

right. Sean Deegan was like junk food: bad for you, but you couldn't refuse him. Mum seemed to mull something over a long time before she spoke again. In the end she appeared to come to the conclusion that it would take something special to win him over.

'Aidan,' she said, 'if I tell you something, you have to promise you will never repeat it. It would break Mark's heart.'

Aidan met her eyes. He feigned defiance but in the end he conceded.

'I promise.'

'I've never loved any man the way I loved Sean, none of the other boyfriends . . .'

Her voice dropped.

'Not even Mark.'

The ground seemed to lurch under Aidan's feet.

'Hang on,' he said. 'Let me get this right, you still love Deegan?'

She nodded.

'I don't want to. Aidan, I'd give anything to feel differently, I really would. You hear all these stupid women saying they like the bad boys, how they make them feel alive, even though they cheat and let you down. I've got nothing but contempt for them but . . .'

She let her arms flop by her sides. 'Looks as if I'm one of them.'

Aidan listened, listened properly for the first time since he'd returned.

'This is really hard, Aidan. I don't even know why I'm telling you. Maybe you're too young to understand, but one day you will meet somebody you just can't get out of your mind.'

He already had.

Jade.

'You pray they will be the one, your soul mate.'

She sighed.

'But what are the chances of that, eh? Anyway, Sean made me feel so alive. When I wasn't with him, I ached for him. I only felt one hundred per cent me when I was with him. Does that make sense?'

Aidan nodded, still thinking of Jade.

'Don't get me wrong, I love Mark. He put me back together after Sean. He brought you up as his own son. He's been a father in every single way. He's a better man than Sean, more honest, more caring, more decent. I know he will never, ever let us down.'

'But?'

'But there's no thrill. He's comfortable like an old dressing gown.'

She smiled, fondness for Mark welling in her look.

'He's like a trusting old dog. It's just . . . he will never make me feel the way Sean does.'

Aidan saw a startled look enter her eyes as she thought of something.

'Don't get me wrong,' she stammered. 'I haven't done anything. I would never betray Mark. It's just . . .'

Aidan waited.

'Though we can never be together, Sean will always be the one.'

All Aidan's resentment fell away then. He felt sorry for her. He should have touched her arm, offered her a hug, anything to tell her it was all right. But he failed her, same way he failed Jade. He could only think about how much he was hurting. Even then, after everything, he knew he was still one selfish brat. Somewhere inside, he sensed what he ought to do. But he couldn't get past the idea that everybody was against him. They were dumping on him. Mum wiped her eyes. A pleading tone came into her voice.

'You won't tell Mark, will you? Tell me you'll never say anything.'

'You really think I'd do that to him?' Aidan complained. 'I've promised, haven't I?

Mum nodded and managed a smile.

'Yes, you have.'

He looked at her.

'Can I ask a question?'

'Yes.'

'How can you live with Dad this way, knowing he's second best?'

She blew her nose and dabbed again at her eyes.

'He cherishes me. He loves you as if you're his natural son. He makes us a family. I *am* happy, in my way.'

She realised she had struck a false note.

'I have a kind of happiness,' she said, correcting herself. 'Aidan, it's like this. No matter what they say in the books, nobody can have it all. If your life is sixty, seventy per cent of what you want it to be, then you're a very lucky person. Lots of people get by on less. So that's me, kind of happy. I can demand it all and destroy everything or I can settle for what I've got and be seventy per cent happy. Do you understand that?' Aidan let Jade fade to the back of his mind and brought Emily's face out of the shadows. Seventy per cent happy, maybe that's what he should settle for.

'Yes, I understand.'

'When we leave tomorrow,' Mum said finally, 'we're going to go back to the way we were. We're going to carry on as though this never happened.'

'Do you think we can do that?' Aidan asked.

'We've got to,' Mum said. 'Ready to go back?'

He nodded.

'Can I borrow your mobile?' he said.
Mum passed it to him and flashed a question.
'I'm going to call Emily.'

The Gunslinger

It's a done deal. The Gunslinger examines the tools
of his trade: the shooter, the bullets. There is one
more tool of his trade: his ruthlessness. He puts all
emotion aside now. He will enjoy the experience for
what it is. He will use the gun. He will glory in its roar.
He will step out of the shadows and soon, when he is
ready to make his move, he will inherit the Earth.

Nine

Aidan wondered if he'd done the right thing. It was turning out to be one of the longest nights of his life and it was going to get a whole lot longer. When he hung up the phone after talking to Emily he felt disappointed. What he had with her, it wasn't even seventy per cent happy – it was nothing. She wasn't Jade.

'Something to eat?' Gran asked.

He laughed. How did the old song go, the one they use in the adverts: *smile though your heart is breaking*. Gran had a new take on it: *eat* though your heart is breaking.

'Did I say something funny?' she asked.

'No, well not on purpose anyway.'

Aidan saw the frown on her face and relented.

'Something to eat, eh? What have you got?'

Gran brightened.

'I bought some nice Eccles cakes. They're made with best butter.'

Best butter. How many people under fifty say that? The Eccles cakes arrived on a plate accompanied by a glass of milk. Gran carried it in on a tray from the Cotswolds, probably a souvenir of one of their coach holidays. Soon, they would be all she had, her souvenirs. Granddad would be gone. She would remember him through her trinkets and photographs. Under her supervision Aidan ate and drank. Sitting there with her watching him he realised that this was her reason for living, to make the people around her feel comfortable, happy and loved. He'd always had her down as a silly old thing. He'd probably treated her cosy respectability with contempt. But he'd seen into the world where Sean Deegan lived. All the money, all the style, and what did he ever do to make anybody feel better? The Eccles cakes tasted good and the milk was cold and refreshing. That's right, Aidan enjoyed his supper. In the movies, when people get hurt they can't eat, can't do anything. Real life isn't necessarily like that. People are living machines. They eat, they sleep, they try to meet their needs. No matter how much you get hurt, no matter how deep the cuts life slashes into your soul, you still get hungry, you go through the motions, you carry on. Mum was carrying on, too. Aidan could hear the hum of her voice in the living room. She was talking to Dad, going through the motions, same way she'd been going through the motions for the last ten, twelve years, however long they'd been together.

'You'll get over it,' Gran said.

Aidan stared. To be honest he wasn't quite sure what she meant. Just how much did she know?

'Yes,' he said, and not just to keep her happy. 'You're right. I'll get over it.'

She squeezed his arm.

'Good lad.'

Time was carrying on too. The kitchen clock said ten. In twelve hours they would be on the M62, heading for the M6 and the South. Then Jade, Sean Deegan and the truth about his family would fade into the northern mist, never to be spoken about again. They would go through the motions.

They would carry on.

Aidan wanted to go to Jade, he just couldn't move. He didn't know how to say sorry. He heard *Newsnight* start in the living room. There Mum and Dad sat, Mum with her secrets, Dad in his naivety. In his front parlour exclusion zone Granddad was probably looking out on the street, thinking of the ghosts of his Liverpool that would tread these pavements until he and his generation were gone. As Aidan sat in the kitchen, the dark eddying up from outside, a thought crawled into his mind: where was Deegan? He tried to imagine him on an Easyjet flight to Barcelona, or on a train south. He didn't believe it though. Quite how he didn't know, but he was sure he hadn't gone. It was so obvious, he had run once, he wasn't about to do it again. He was going to fight to the end for his turf. He had no other life but his gear, his deals, his fight for a share of the action. So Aidan made his decision. He would slip out. One last time he would go out into Elmwood, look for the blue BMW, confront the secret of his past. And that's what he did. He turned the key and went.

The dark rushed up to greet him. It gripped him like black clingfilm, folded him in its tepid grasp. It claimed him for its own. The streets were blurry with fine drizzle, but warm and dank. It was an uncomfortable night, prickling with the neurotic heat that comes before a storm. Aidan walked down Elmwood until he was standing opposite Jade's house. There was a light on in her room. He found himself wondering what she was doing. But they'd said their goodbyes. There was no way back, he knew that. After about ten minutes Mum and Dad appeared at the front door of number 66, looking up and down. He heard his name. He didn't answer. It was as if it was all happening behind a glass screen. Then they were driving towards him. Aidan shrank into the shadows and let them pass. His business was with Sean Deegan.

Another half hour and he was beginning to think he was wrong. Deegan had gone. He could get back to his old life, spend a summer chilling with Emily, Chris and Debs, aim for his share of seventy per cent happiness. That's when he saw a car. Not the blue BMW, not after the way Geraghty's hit man had shot it up. It was a Golf GTI that had swung into the road. Aidan recognised Tony Morrissey at the wheel and Sean Deegan by his side. I knew it, he thought. You couldn't let it go, could you?

It wasn't long before Deegan saw him. The Golf drew up and the passenger window slid down.

'What brings you out at this time?' he asked.

Aidan's eyes flicked across to Tony, then back to Deegan.

'You.'

'How did you know I was going to stay?'

'I knew, that's all.'

Deegan nodded.

'You wait here, Tone,' Deegan said. 'I'm going to talk to my boy.'

They got as far as the Overhead Railway.

'So I'm your boy, am I?' Aidan said.

'I want you to be.'

Aidan shook his head.

'How's that? Are you going to come down to Surrey, take me out for a pizza one weekend out of four? Do you think it's that easy?'

Deegan frowned.

'I don't really know how it is, Aidan. I just want to get to know you.'

'Is that why you came?'

Deegan didn't seem to know the answer to that one.

'I didn't have a plan. I just wanted to talk to you . . . and Jill.'

That's when the scales fell from Aidan's eyes. All that stuff Deegan had said yesterday, he'd never had any intention of walking away. Just one more lousy lie.

'You've got to be crazy!' Aidan yelled. 'What are you going to say to her?'

'You, me and your mother, we can still have something good.'

If Aidan had ever been drawn to Deegan's world, that was the moment he turned away.

'Go away,' Aidan said, revolted. 'How dare you? Just go away. Before you do more damage.'

Deegan's face was unreadable. One thing was clear – he wasn't going anywhere. Aidan looked past him at Tony Morrissey. For once Tony seemed interested in them. That deadpan face of his looked almost anxious. Aidan didn't get it. What did he have to worry about?

'You've got to go,' Aidan repeated. 'You're not going to wreck things for Mum and Dad.'

'I'm your dad.'

Aidan finally drew his line in the sand. He knew what he had, and that was his family. Sean Deegan just didn't figure.

'No you're not,' Aidan told him. 'Mark is. He's always been there. He's my dad because I want him to be.'

Deegan's eyes flashed.

'I'm your blood, Aidan. You can't just forget that.'

'You're right,' Aidan said. 'I can't. You'll always be there . . .'

He went to interrupt. Aidan waved the protest away.

'But you didn't make me the way I am. Mum did, Mark did. I'm not defined by you. If you'd never come back, I'd still be the way I am now. Listen to me, if you care at all about me, you'll leave my family alone. Whatever you think you had thirteen years ago, it's not there any more. You blew it. You can't go back.' Aidan glanced at Tony, but he had turned away. He was staring down at something. Aidan looked Deegan in the eye.

'Just go, will you?' he said.

'You're sure that's what you want?'

'I'm sure.'

'Final answer?'

'Who do you think you are?' Aidan said, almost tempted to laugh. 'Chris Tarrant?'

'Final answer?' Deegan said stubbornly, immune to Aidan's sense of humour.

'Yes,' Aidan said. 'Final answer.'

Deegan's broad, heavy shoulders sagged just a little. Despite all the bad things he'd done, he was still human, and just then his insides were being ripped apart. Aidan let him reach the car then he followed him.

'I don't hate you,' he said.

Deegan met his look for a moment then slid into the passenger seat. Aidan saw Tony still staring down the way he had the first time Aidan saw him. What was he doing? Then Aidan had it. It was a book with a grey-bronze cover, a Stephen King. Funny, he thought, I never had Tony Morrissey down as a reader.

'Thanks for that, at least,' Deegan said, breaking in on Aidan's thought.

He didn't think Deegan was being sarcastic. There was no time to make his mind up. Mum and Dad had returned. Aidan saw Mum getting out and moving towards him. She wasn't the only one. The front door of number 66 was open again. Granddad's fragile frame was caught in the light of the hallway.

'You won't see me again,' Deegan said, barely acknowledging their presence. 'Have a good life, Aidan.'

It was as he pulled away that Aidan remembered Tony's book. You only need the tiniest detail to recognise something. That book, he'd read it himself, in the same edition too, *The Dark Tower*, part one, *The Gunslinger*. A stream of terror coursed down Aidan's spine. In an instant he made the link. The Gunslinger. A wave of realisation swept over him. Why hadn't he recognised that grey-bronze cover earlier? He had seen Tony reading, he had seen the book, but he hadn't understood. The first line, how did it go? It was something about a man in black, yes, a man in black fleeing across the desert.

'And the Gunslinger followed,' Aidan said out loud, remembering how the book started.

The Gunslinger followed.

Aidan heard a voice screaming one word over and over again:

'Dad! Dad! Dad!'

The voice was his own. He saw Deegan's head snap round. One thing he would remember later, the tendons in his neck were standing out like steel rods. He knew the truth even before Aidan yelled it down the street.

'Dad!' Aidan cried. 'It wasn't the Scotsman. It's him. The Gunslinger, it's Morrissey.' His heart was slamming with horror. Don't let him die. Please God, don't let him die. But that's when the night exploded into madness. Two figures were struggling in the car. The Golf went out of control, bouncing onto the pavement. The scream rose in Aidan's throat a third time.

'Dad!'

He was running. He felt Mum's hand on his arm but he shrugged it away. Like the dream, it was just like the dream.

'Dad!'

He was too late. From inside the car there was a roar of cordite and metal. A spasm of utter helplessness and despair shuddered through Aidan.

'No!'

He was to learn later that a bullet had crashed through Deegan's ribcage, spraying fragments of metal through lung, muscle and bone. Another had torn a gouge out of his throat, like a plug letting the lifeblood drain away in a hot, red stream. The passenger door swung open and Deegan fell sprawling on the pavement. He was still alive when Aidan reached him but his eyes were shocked and unfocused. Blood was pumping from his neck. Aidan's hands flew to the wound as he tried helplessly to staunch the blood. Nothing he did made any difference. The dark streams found their way through his fingers. Aidan knew Deegan was dying. Voices bounced around him. Hands tugged at him.

'It's no good, Aidan. He's gone.'

Aidan was rising on wobbly legs, his eyes blurred with tears, when he saw Morrissey stumble out onto the road. He too was hurt. Aidan saw the killer, then he saw his weapon. His arm was torn and bloody and he had dropped the gun. Desolate, burning with hatred, Aidan was on it in an instant. He felt the revolver cold and heavy in his hand.

'You killed him,' Aidan yelled. 'Murderer!'

Morrissey's face floated at the end of the gun. Aidan only had to squeeze the trigger and justice would be done.

'Put it down,' came a voice. 'Aidan, please.'

The voice was Mum's.

'He killed . . .' Aidan panted.

He trained the gun on Morrissey. '*You* killed him.'

Morrissey was sinking to the ground, blood soaking his shirt. Nothing anybody could say was going to make any difference. Vengeance. An eye for an eye. Justice. Aidan could hear the siren of a police car in the distance. He had to do it now.

'You've got to die.'

The Gunslinger's face slackened. Fear was there, and resignation. Aidan would have done it too. He would have killed Morrissey there, on the street where he had started to find out who he was. It was a dead man who stopped him.

'No, Aidan,' Granddad said, stepping between them.

'Get out of the way!' Aidan yelled.

'There isn't much left of me,' Granddad said. 'My life isn't worth anything any more.'

He glanced down at Tony Morrissey trying to crawl away, leaving a trail of blood on the pavement.

'You never know, if you put a bullet through me, it might just hit this piece of trash too. Your choice, Aidan. It won't make much difference either way.'

'Granddad, stop it.'

Granddad held out his hand.

'The gun, Aidan.'

'Why are you protecting him?' Aidan cried.

The gun was shaking in his hand.

'I'm not,' Granddad said. 'It's you I'm doing it for. I love you, lad. I love you so much it hurts. Don't throw your life away for Sean Deegan. He isn't worth it. You're everything he never could be. You've got a future. You can be happy.'

Happy. Not seventy per cent happy. Happy. Just happy. Suddenly the gun was heavy in Aidan's hand. He let his arm fall. Granddad took the gun and put an almost weightless arm round him.

'Come inside,' he said. 'Let the police do their work.'

Until that moment Aidan had barely registered their arrival: the flashing blue lights, the flak-jacketed officers. Police and paramedics surrounded Morrissey. It was over.

Ten

They stayed for Deegan's funeral. Aidan made a big effort that day. He knew he had hurt Mark. He had called Deegan 'Dad' there on the street as Tony Morrissey's gun ripped him apart. Aidan knew that was a lie. He'd meant everything he had said to Deegan. Mark had raised him. He'd taught Aidan his values, his outlook on the world. Maybe Aidan would make them his own, maybe he would rebel against them; either way they were poles within which he would make his decisions. Deegan didn't have any say in the matter. He'd given his boy life. Which direction that life would take was out of his hands. Since the day he had killed a man thirteen years before, it always had been.

The funeral took place at 1.15pm on a warm, slightly overcast day at the end of July at Our Lady, Blessed Queen of Peace. There were as many press as mourners. The Liverpool Echo would make it the lead story the next day. *Death of a gangster*, that was the headline. One section of the report would stay in Aidan's mind for good. *There have been other gangster funerals in this city*, it read. *The mourners come in their hundreds. Their livelihoods have depended on the man being buried. But the mourners only come when the dynasty continues, when there is something to be had from allegiance to the family. In Sean Deegan's case this wasn't true. In Liverpool's gang wars he was a loser. He was buried virtually unmourned.*

It was true. Deegan's mother and sister were there. That was it for family. Then there were Mum, Dad and Aidan. The two groups had nothing to say to each other. They sat apart. So that's all there were to say goodbye to Sean Deegan: five people, six including the priest. Father McCann did what he had to do, no more. There was no eulogy. There was one wreath, the one from Deegan's mother and sister. It said: Sean. Mum asked Aidan if he wanted to send a wreath. He said no.

They sat in the cold, dark church watching the dust motes dropping through the watery, slanting sunlight, then trudged out to see the coffin lowered into the earth. Mrs Deegan cried. The rest, even his sister, stood dry-eyed, slightly embarrassed by the one unequivocal and real show of emotion in the whole service. Finally, without even saying goodbye to the other two mourners, the Shaw family walked to their car and drove back to Elmwood to bid their last, brief farewells to Gran and Granddad. As they turned at the top of the street Aidan craned his neck to look back, hoping against hope that he would catch sight of Jade standing at her front door watching him go. She wasn't there.

Aidan had his summer with Emily, but his heart wasn't in it. It didn't take Emily long to work that out. She soon started asking if there was somebody else, if something had happened in Liverpool, something other than the death of Sean Deegan. Always the coward, Aidan assured her it hadn't. He was still after his seventy per cent happiness. But he was kidding himself. He never came close. It took months to happen, but they drifted apart in the end. Aidan had other girlfriends, of course he did, but there was nobody special, nobody that mattered. He went through the motions.

That could be said of life at home too. They did the usual family stuff but they were never quite as close as they had been before that trip to Liverpool. Nothing big seemed to change, nothing you could put your finger on. There was a change in atmosphere though. They were never really easy with each other after that summer. They lived with their secrets, skirted them, referred to them in code. What they never did was confront them, go into how they really felt. There might be more skeletons to come. They came to an unspoken agreement to leave them there. Aidan had always been the one who wanted the truth. Not any more. He'd come to understand that a few lies, or at least the quiet avoidance of the truth, can be the dividing line between muddling through and falling apart.

One winter's day, four months after Deegan was killed, they drove north again. They watched the lights of Liverpool dancing before them. They had come to bury Granddad. He finally succumbed to his illness three weeks before Christmas. His funeral was a different affair to Deegan's. The church, the same one that said goodbye to Sean Deegan, was packed to overflowing. There were people there who loved him and respected him. Patricia had come over from the States with her family. Some of his old workmates turned up. As the cortege pulled away from the church parishioners lined the route in the street outside. Four of Granddad's closest friends helped Mark and Aidan carry the coffin. The rest marched behind with their old trade union banner snapping in the wind.

'Poor old beggars,' Dad said. 'They still think they're fighting the class struggle. Dinosaurs.'

'The point is,' Gran said, reproaching him, 'they stand for something. They still care for what Joe cared for. They remember what this city was. They dream of what it can be.'

It was the longest speech she had ever made. Dad didn't know what to say to that, or maybe he did but didn't think it was the time or place. He shook the hands of every man. He might not agree with them. He might even think they were ridiculous, but there was a grudging kind of respect all the same. He saw in them a basic honesty and decency he couldn't help but admire.

'I feel like a fish out of water,' he told Mum back at the house as people ate and drank and discussed old times.

'It'll be over soon,' she said, patting his arm reassuringly. She caught Aidan's eye.

'If it wasn't for your Granddad,' she said, 'we might not be together now.'

That was the moment their relationship started to mend.

While Aidan was there he asked after Jade. Her baby was due sometime in the New Year.

'You're not going to see her, are you?' Gran asked.

Aidan shook his head.

'No, we've nothing to say to each other.'

Gran still wasn't appeased.

'You promise you'll keep away?'

'Yes, I promise.'

She relaxed.

'I'm pleased to hear it.'

Aidan kept his promise. He was only there that one night. By the time the last of the mourners had gone there was only time to clear up after them, watch a little late night TV and go to bed. Aidan stayed away from Jade. It didn't stop him thinking about her long into the early hours.

Epilogue

Jade has never left Aidan. He did well in his GCSEs, went on to do four A levels and spend three years at university. He had his share of girlfriends. For long periods he even seemed to forget about Jade. But there was always something that would bring her face shimmering up from the past. The slightest thing could do it: a breeze, the way a certain girl tossed her hair, the way another one walked. Jade was always there. Maybe Jade is what brought him back. Seven years after the summer that changed his life, the way he looked at the world, Aidan took the decision to go back to Liverpool. He found the city changed, or at least changing. There was a buzz in the air. It had won City of Culture status. There was reason to believe in the future. It would be pushing it too far to say he was going home, but it was a kind of return. The place had got under his skin. He stayed with Gran while he settled into his new job. He works on the *Liverpool Echo*, a job which gives him access to the city's two souls. He has reported on gangland slayings. Two names he recognised immediately from the archives. Morrissey was pictured recently at his father's funeral. He has another eight years to serve. Dave Geraghty is dead, victim of a drive-by shooting in Bootle. Carrying on the family business from six feet under. Aidan has equally written about the stirrings of economic revival in the city.

Finally, after three months at 66 Elmwood Street, he found himself a flat and moved out. Gran was sad to see him go but he goes round for his tea once a week and she treats him to a feast. Returning to Elmwood didn't put him back in touch with Jade. What he learned about her came from neighbours. They told him what they knew. Her mum finally found herself a man who would stand by her. She went to live with him in Maghull. They are still happy. Jade got herself a small house in Walton. Aidan gathered a few bits of information about her. She wasn't in a relationship. She lived for her child, a daughter by the name of Tess. Aidan guessed she named her after Tess of the D'Urbervilles. She was a good mother, even Gran gave her that. She'd even let the fake tan fade, from what people told him. Aidan couldn't help but wonder what she looked like pale.

Paul Gorman wasn't on the scene any more. He did two stretches in Walton Prison, the first for Actual Bodily Harm, the second for drugs offences. The last anybody heard of him, he was in the Royal Liverpool Hospital recovering from a stabbing. Aidan has been sitting here in the living room all afternoon, thinking about Jade, remembering that summer. There's a little piece of paper in his closed fist. It has her address on it. He got it from one of her friends. The question is: does he open his fist and read it, or does he drop it in the waste paper bin and get on with his life? Work is good. He's doing something he enjoys and his colleagues are a good bunch. There is no need to go back. People always tell you it's a bad idea, going back. Things are never the same. Years ago Aidan wondered whether to go to Jade. He made his decision then. They had nothing to say to each other.

So what's changed? They're older for starters, maybe even wiser. A lot of water has flowed under the bridge. There are bound to be recriminations. Aidan walked out on her, didn't he? That's it then. Drop the note in the bin. Forget her, Aidan. Get on with your life. It's only sensible. The thing is, he doesn't want to be sensible any more. He's done that. He got his education. He's found himself a job so he could pay off his student loan. What he wants to be is happy.

But why would he want Jade back? Why would he want to bring up another man's kid? Who needs that much grief? Aidan, that's who. Because there's only one person who ever offered him the chance of happiness, not the seventy per cent, the whole thing. They fought, they argued, but with Jade he was more alive than he has ever been with another human being. Finally, he opens his fist. He takes the scrap of paper and he reads the address. Maybe he won't get past the front door. Maybe she'll scream and shout and send him on his way. It's about all he deserves. Maybe they really don't have anything to say to each other.

But he has to try.

He has to take this one chance to be happy.

Also by Alan Gibbons

The Edge

Danny is a boy on the edge. A boy teetering on the brink of no return, living in fear.

Cathy is his mother. She's been broken by fear.

Chris Kane is fear – and they belong to him.

But one day they escape. They're looking for freedom, for the promised land where they can start really living. Instead they find prejudice, and danger of another kind.

Uncompromising and disturbing, but utterly readable, Alan Gibbons' latest novel positively crackles with tension as he writes about a mother and her son desperate to start a new life.

Shortlisted for the Carnegie Medal.

Caught in the Crossfire

'You know what happens to people like you? You get hit in the crossfire.'

Shockwaves sweep the world in the aftermath of 11 September. The Patriotic League barely need an excuse in their fight to get Britain back for the British, but this is chillingly perfect.

Rabia and Tahir are British Muslims, Daz and Jason are out looking for trouble, Mike and Liam are brothers on different sides. None of them will escape unscarred from the terrifying and tragic events which will weave their lives together.

Marking a new dimension in his writing on race, riots and real life *Caught in the Crossfire* is an unforgettable novel that Alan Gibbons needed to write.

The Dark Beneath

'Today I shot the girl I love.'

GCSE's are over and sixteen-year-old Imogen is looking forward to a perfect, lazy English summer. But her world is turned upside down by three refugees, all hiding from life. Anthony is fourteen, already an outcast, bullied and shunned by his peers. Farid is an asylum seeker from Afghanistan, who has travelled across continents seeking peace. And Gordon Craig is a bitter, lonely man. She knows all of them, but she doesn't know how dangerous they are. Being part of their lives could cost Imogen her own.

Supercharged with tension and drama, Alan Gibbon's novel is about what happens when the fabric of normality is ripped apart exposing the terrifying dark beneath.

The Defender

When Kenny Kincaid turns his back on the past he has no idea of the legacy he is bequeathing his only son, Ian.

Was he escaping from the paramilitaries, from too much violence and bloodshed, too many victims? Or was he betraying the Cause, turning his back on his comrades-in-arms when he fled clutching his baby son and quarter of a million pounds from a bank job? They think so, and they're intent on revenge. Years later Kenny is still a target – and now so is Ian.

Father and son are going to have to live with it . . . or die with it.

Controversial and compulsive reading, this is an unputdownable thriller.

'Alan Gibbons can always be relied upon to raise pulse rates, and his *The Defender* is . . . achingly exciting'
Independent

The Lost Boys' Appreciation Society

Something was wrong. The anger-flash had drained out of Dad's face, replaced by a blank pallor.

Like disbelief . . .

When Mum was killed in a car crash our lives were wrecked too.

Gary, John and Dad are lost without Mum. Gary is only 14 and goes seriously off the rails, teetering on the brink of being on the wrong side of the law. John is wrestling with GCSEs and his first romance – but he's carrying the burden of trying to cope with Gary and Dad at the same time. And they're all living with the memories of someone they can never replace.

Alan Gibbons writes with compassion – and flashes of humour – about surviving against all the odds.

The Shadow of the Minotaur

'Real life' or the death defying adventures of the Greek myths, with their heroes and monsters, daring deeds and narrow escapes – which would you choose?

For Phoenix it's easy. He hates his new home and the new school where he is bullied. He's embarrassed by his computer geek dad. But when he logs on to the Legendeer, the game his dad is working on, he can be a hero. He is Theseus fighting the terrifying Minotaur, or Perseus battling with snake-haired Medusa.

The trouble is The Legendeer is more than just a game. Play it if you dare.

Vampyr Legion

What if there are real worlds where our nightmares live and wait for us?

Phoenix has found one and it's alive. Armies of bloodsucking vampyrs and terrifying werewolves, the creatures of our darkest dreams, are poised to invade our world.

But Phoenix has encountered the creator of *Vampyr Legion*, the evil Gamesmaster, before and knows that this deadly computer game is for real – he must win or never come back.

Warriors of the Raven

The game opens up the gateway between our world and the world of the myths.

The Gamesmaster almost has our world at his mercy. Twice before fourteen-year-old Phoenix has battled against him in *Shadow of the Minotaur* and *Vampyr Legion*, but Warriors of the Raven is the game at its most complex and deadly level. This time, Phoenix enters the arena for the final conflict, set in the world of Norse myth. Join Phoenix in Asgard to fight Loki, the Mischief-maker, the terrifying Valkyries, dragons and fire demons – and hope for victory. Our future depends on him.

Julie and Me . . . and Michael Owen Makes Three

It's been a year of own goals for Terry.

– Man U, the entire focus of his life (what else is there?), lose to arch-enemies Liverpool FC

– he looks like Chris Evans, no pecs

– Mum and Dad split up (just another statistic)

– he falls seriously in love with drop dead gorgeous Julie. It's bad enough watching Frisky Fitzy (school golden boy) drool all over her, but worse still she's an ardent Liverpool FC supporter.

Life as Terry knows it is about to change in this hilariously funny, sometimes sad, utterly readable modern Romeo and Juliet story.

Julie and Me: Treble Trouble

For one disastrous year Terry has watched Julie, the girl of his dreams, go out with arch rival Frisky Fitz, seen his Mum and Dad's marriage crumble and his beloved Man U go the same way. 2001 has got to be better.

– Will he get to run his hands through the lovely Julie's raven tresses?

– What happens when his new streamlined Mum gets a life?

– Can Man U redeem themselves and do the business in the face of the impossible?

Returning the love – that's what it's all about.

Read the concluding part of *Julie and Me* and all will be revealed.